BE WITH ME

A DARK CONTEMPORARY STAND ALONE NOVEL

ANGEL RAYNE

ALSO BY ANGEL RAYNE

Mafia Romance Reading Order

Luca and Veda

His Game

His Stakes

His Win

Stand Alone Novels

Tyler and Ailee

Be With Me

SYNOPSIS

I'm not her knight in shining armor. I'm her downfall. She just doesn't know it yet.

When I'm not in school, I make extra cash working as a model.
My favorite photographer to work with?
Ailee Walsh.
And not just because she's so sexy she should be in the shots with me.
Although that reason is definitely up there.
With her dark hair and white skin, Ailee reminds me of a princess.
The woman makes my head swim and my stomach tangle up in ropes.
Not to mention what she does to other parts of me...
The last time I saw her, she was married. So I did my job and left.
However, I never stopped thinking about her. Not once.
Now, a year later, the ring on her finger is gone.
There's nothing stopping me from going after what I want.
Not even the destructive road my life is on...

Being with Ailee would be like a fairytale.
Too bad I'm no fucking prince.

PROLOGUE

Tyler

Eight Months Ago

I blinked against the bright glare of a streetlight, gagging on the stench in the air. When my eyes adjusted and I could focus, I looked around, trying to figure out where the fuck I was.

There was a hard brick wall digging into my back where I was slumped against it, and in front of me was some sort of large metal container. Bags that reeked like rotten food and God knew what else overflowed the top and hid me from anyone who might happen to come along.

I took stock of my body, searching for injuries. I felt a little beaten up, but otherwise, I seemed to be okay.

When I could manage it, I crawled out of the piles of trash. It was dark, the alley lit only by that damn streetlight. I felt around in my pockets for my cell phone. I had no fucking idea what time it was, or even what day. What I did know was my head felt like it was about to explode, and I hoped like hell no one I knew would see me like this. I had no recollection of going out, or of drinking, but if the taste of death in my mouth was any indication, that's exactly what I'd been doing.

Shaken up, more than a little disoriented, and still searching for my phone, I wracked my brain trying to remember what the fuck had happened. But nothing came to me. It was like I'd lost time somehow. My heart began to pound and a sheen of sweat broke out across my skin despite the cool temperature. I was fucking terrified, my pulse rising to near heart attack levels, when this little tan dog came trotting up to me with his tail wagging and his tongue hanging out of his mouth.

He looked so happy to see me, greeting me like he'd been waiting for me for hours, that I forgot my own issues, if only for a moment or two. I looked around again, expecting his owner to come around the corner looking for him, but no one ever did. I checked for a collar, but he had no tags.

I bent over to pet him, and as I rubbed his soft head, I sagged against the side of the building. Gradually, the pounding in my ears began to slow to a more normal beat.

Dogs, man. We didn't deserve them.

After a while, I tried to get him to go home, assuring him I had nothing on me he would want. He didn't seem to believe me, though, so eventually I gave up trying to convince him to leave and just let him hang out. Patting down my pockets and kicking the trash around on the ground, I tried one more time to find my phone, but it wasn't on me. And I had no idea where I'd left it.

With a groan, I looked down at the dog. "What the actual fuck happened here?" I asked him.

He cocked his head but seemed as clueless as I was.

I pressed the heels of my hands against my pounding temples. My voice sounded like I'd been screaming all night and my eyes burned like hell, so I closed them as I tried to get my shit together. When I opened them again, my new friend was still there. "I feel like shit," I told him.

The dog tilted his head to the other side this time, like he was listening to what I was saying. Then he ran off. I thought maybe he'd finally came to his senses and realized I had no food for him. But a few seconds later, he was back.

With a Snickers bar in his mouth.

Full-sized, too. None of that bite-sized crap.

He dropped it at my feet and barked. I eyed up the candy through eyes that were squinted against the pain in my head, and my stomach growled like I hadn't eaten in a week. And for all I knew, I hadn't. But still... "Sorry, man.

I appreciate the offer, but I don't know where you got that or what might be in it. So, I'm gonna pass."

I left the candy bar there. To my right, I saw a street, and I staggered in that direction. Above me, thunder rattled the sky, and I covered my ears in an effort to keep my head from pounding along with the wheels of the light rail. When I made it to the end of the alley, I could see I was in a bad area of Belltown. Okay. I made my way down the main street until I could flag down a taxi to take me home. Luckily, my wallet was still in my back pocket.

The pup followed me out to the road, sitting beside me as I waited for my ride like he belonged there. And when the taxi pulled over, he let out this pathetic little whine, giving me the biggest, saddest, puppy dog eyes I'd ever seen in my life.

I eyed him as I stood there with the back door open. I wanted to help him, but as I was recently discovering I could barely take care of myself.

However, at the thought of leaving him there and heading home to spend the rest of the night alone, my heart picked up again, beating so fast and hard I swayed on my feet.

Finally, I took a deep breath and gave in. "You wanna come?"

That was all the invitation he needed. With a happy grin on his furry face and his tongue lolling out, he hopped into the back, sitting on the seat like he did this sort of thing all the time. Climbing in behind him, I gave the driver directions to my apartment, and we went home.

Later the next day, I found out I'd been MIA for two days.

This was the first time that had ever happened to me. I lost five more days and spent hundreds on doctor copays over the next three months, trying to figure out why I couldn't remember going out or why I would black out when I didn't remember drinking. I was tested for every physical ailment under the sun. No one could tell me what had happened, or why, and eventually, I just gave up.

Determined not to spend my life agonizing over a few weird days, I pushed the memories—or lack thereof—to the back of mind and forgot about them.

Not so much the dog, though.

Nah. He stayed with me.

CHAPTER 1

Tyler

I was going to see Ailee again. After almost a year, I was finally going to see her again. And honestly, I wasn't quite sure how I felt about it.

Excited, for sure. Scared? Yeah, a little. Hungry?

Fuck yes.

But not in a cannibalistic kind of way. I'm not a psycho. However, Ailee Walsh was—hands down—one of the most delicious women I'd ever had the honor of meeting. She was...everything. Just fucking everything. Her sparkling eyes were as blue as a cloudless sky, and the way they danced when she laughed made me think of the warm, carefree summer days I'd seen in movies, but I'd never had the opportunity to experience. Not even when I was a kid.

She also had a smile that made my heart pound in my chest. And a voluptuous, old Hollywood figure that girls —and a lot of guys—these days just didn't appreciate. It wasn't their fault. Every fucking media outlet out there told them the only way they'd be attractive was to be as thin and wafer-like as possible.

But me? I was a man who liked a woman that filled up the space between my arms. A woman I could sink into and lose myself in without worrying about breaking one of her fragile bones.

God, I sounded like a fucking Hallmark commercial. And I probably looked like I belonged in one as I stared out my kitchen window, the perfect picture of one of the characters in those movies my mom was always watching. But as cheesy as I sounded, even to myself, it was all true, what I thought about her. Hell, I was getting hard just thinking about it.

And, I'd just heard she'd recently gotten divorced.

Something cold and wet hit the back of my knee, bringing my thoughts back to the fact that I had a modeling appointment with Ailee, the only photographer I've ever felt self-conscience around. With a shaking hand, I set down my new cell phone on the counter and found Snickers sitting behind me. I gave him a smile, leaning over to rub his long, soft ears. "Hey, buddy. Where ya been?" My dog licked my hand as I tried to brush dirt from his creamy white muzzle.

My phone chimed again, and I gave my pup one last pat before I straightened up to see a text from Stefanie, the romance author who'd just booked me for her new cover. She said she'd heard back from Ailee and we were good to go for the date she'd told me, exactly two weeks from now. I texted her back, thanking her for thinking of me and assuring her I had it on my calendar and that I would be there.

There was no fucking way I would miss it. And not just because I desperately needed the money.

Phone still in my hand, I sat down hard, nearly missing the chair I'd yanked out from beneath the kitchen table. A shiver ran over me, and it had nothing to do with the fact that I was wearing nothing but dark blue boxer briefs. My first-floor apartment was warm, but I refused to turn on the A/C. It was nearly fall, the weather should be cooling down by now, and I wasn't about to blow money I didn't have on a high electric bill.

Glancing at the time on the microwave, I took a steadying breath and got my ass in gear. I was supposed to be at that new restaurant near Pike Place in thirty minutes, and I didn't think the restaurant would let Willow hold our table if I wasn't there. I threw on a nice shirt and a pair of jeans, tugged my cleanest pair of sneakers on, and searched frantically for my wallet. I found it on the counter and shoved it and my phone into my back pockets. I wasn't worried about leaving Snickers, he was already curled up in his favorite spot on the couch by the time I left. I closed the patio door that I normally left open for him so he could go muck around in the courtyard at will, smiling at the sound of his soft snores, and then I locked him in and went to go meet my foster sister.

She was already there when I arrived, standing near the door. Tall and slender, she reminded me very much of her namesake with her pale skin, and her light-colored hair that rose from her scalp and dangled in wispy curls just past her shoulders. "Hey." I greeted her with a kiss on the cheek. "Sorry, the bus was running late."

My excuse was met with the "arched brow of disbelief" and blank stare I'd been receiving since we were kids. "More like you forgot about our date until the last minute, then you threw on the first shirt you found in your closet, grabbed a pair of jeans from the semi-clean pile, and ran out the door."

I grinned at her.

"Did you at least feed Snickers before you left?"

"Nah," I told her. "He was snoring on the couch when I left. I'll feed him when I get home."

"Don't forget, you still need to get me a key," she reminded me as the hostess led us to our table.

I had forgotten. But it was no big deal. We always had keys to each other's place, ever since we'd both moved to Seattle. I'd agreed it was a good idea. It was just easier if either one of us had to pet sit or whatever, even though her damn cat still didn't like me. "I've only been in the new apartment a few weeks. I'll get one made this weekend."

I opened the menu the hostess had given us and started checking out what was there. The place looked like a fusion of Mexican food and Thai food. Interesting. The waiter came over and I ordered an iced tea, then went back to studying the menu.

"All right. What's up with you?"

I looked at Willow over the top of my menu. "Me?"

She rolled her eyes. "Yeah, you. Either your leg is possessed, or you've suddenly got some kind of major nervous tick. You're jostling the whole table, Ty, and you haven't sat still for two seconds since you got here. So, what's up?"

I hid behind my menu again. We'd known each other most of our lives. There was no way I'd be able to look her in the eye and deny I was nervous. And I could say for certain that it wasn't going to get any better as the day I was going to see Ailee again got closer and closer. And that right there was ammunition my sister did NOT need to know. "Nothin'. I got a call for a shoot right before I came here. I'm just a little nervous."

My menu was yanked from my hands and slapped down flat onto the table. "Bullshit. You never get nervous about shoots. And this is how I know you're lying to me. Which you also can't do well. So, you might as well fess up now."

I grinned at her. I couldn't help it. "Or, what? You'll call Mom and tell on me?"

She smiled sweetly for a brief second, right before she whipped out her cell phone from her purse and made like she was doing exactly that.

I laughed. "Knock it off. You know damn well you're not calling anyone."

Willow turned the phone around so I could see. The word "Mom" and our foster mother's phone number lit up the screen, and it was ringing. I tried to grab it from her, but she pulled it away just in time. "You're such a fucking brat." I laughed.

"Hi, Mom!" she said a moment later. I could hear our foster mother's southern drawl on the other end. Willow winked at me. "I'm good." She paused as the woman, who was our mother for all intents and purposes, fired off the usual questions. "Yeah, I'm still working at the craft shop. Nope, still not dating anyone." Another pause. "Because I'm tired of men and all the girls at work are straight." She grinned at me. "So, Tyler's here. Uh huh. Yup." Her face screwed up in thought. "I'm not sure." She dragged out the words, adding a touch of drama to her show. "He seems to be okay, but he's really nervous about something and won't tell me what it is." Another pause. "Sure. Okay. Yup. Love you, too." With a look of triumph, she held the phone out to me.

I made no move to take it. "Really?" I asked her.

"Tyler, you better pick up the phone." Our mother's laughing voice could barely be heard above the energetic music playing through the speakers in the ceiling.

I rolled my eyes, much to Willow's amusement, and took the phone from her outstretched hand. "Hi, Mom."

"Honey, why do you tease your sister like that?"

"Because it's fun." I stuck my tongue out at Willow like I used to do when we were younger. She was a few years older and came from a completely different background. But once we'd both gotten comfortable in our new home, we'd grown up just like any two siblings. And that included me getting away with murder while she got stuck cleaning the house—when she wasn't bogged down with homework, anyway. Willow had taken all advanced classes through high school and college, graduating with a double major in law and political science. So why she worked in a craft store was a mystery none of us knew the answer to.

I chatted with my foster mother, not realizing until just this moment how much I'd missed her and our foster dad. They lived in the northern part of Texas near Amarillo, and that's where we'd grown up. As the only two kids in the house, my sister and I had grown close. When I'd decided to move to Seattle a few years ago, Willow had decided to come with me. We'd roomed together for the first year, until she met her ex-boyfriend and moved in with him, leaving me with the apartment all to myself. After they broke it off, she chose to stay on her own, although she was never very far away. And out of necessity, I'd found a smaller, cheaper apartment near Pioneer Square. I'd just got settled in right before I found Snickers. It was good that my new place allowed pets.

After reassuring my mom that all was okay and catching her up on what was happening in my life—at least the happy, abbreviated version—I hung up right as the waitress showed up to take our orders. "I can't believe you did that to me," I shot at her when we were alone again.

Willow wasn't affected by my attempt at anger. She waved a hand in the air. "Pfft. Whatever. You need to call home more."

She was absolutely right. However, that wasn't the point. "You're lucky we're in a public place."

"Or what?" Her eyes narrowed, and she was once again the ten-year-old girl who'd dared me to stop her from snooping through my stuff.

I shook my head, fighting the urge to smile. I was unable to stay upset with the only stable person in my life. "Don't you have someone else to harass?"

"Nope," she answered cheerfully. "Just you."

"Great." I sighed dramatically.

"So, who are you shooting for?"

I rubbed the back of my neck. "Uh, that author Stefanie Heathers."

"Didn't you work with her before?"

"Yeah, last year." I looked around the restaurant, checking out the other patrons and the décor, hoping like hell she'd drop it. "Have you heard from the loser again?"

Hazel eyes that tilted up at the corners, accentuated by eyeliner, narrowed in on me again. She completely ignored my question about her ex. "You really are nervous about this shoot." Resting her arms on the table, she leaned in. "The question is, why? I know it's not the author. Or what she plans to do with your photo. You've been on lots of romance covers."

"Let it go, Willow."

Again, she completely ignored me. Per the usual. "Who's the photographer?"

The back of my neck burned, and I rubbed it again. "I don't know. Who cares?"

A look of satisfaction crossed her face, and she sat back in her chair. "Well, as I know for a fact that you're completely straight, there's only one female photographer —that I know of—that you've worked with before, and that's the chick who did the last cover Stefanie Heathers wanted, isn't it?"

"She's not a 'chick,' Willow. She's a professional photographer."

"I'm right! Aren't I? It's the photographer chick you're nervous about seeing!" She practically crowed with delight at figuring me out.

I threw up my hands. "Fine. Yes. Okay? Are you happy now?"

All signs of teasing fell from her face. "Are you going to ask her out?"

"No!" Then I shrugged. "I don't know. Maybe." At the thought of being alone with Ailee, my blood raced through my body until I felt lightheaded. I looked at my sister and dropped all sense of pretense. It was no use anyway. "She's not like other women." I didn't know how else to explain it.

"Is she single?"

"I think so, yeah. I heard she just got divorced by one of the other cover models who called me for a reference a few weeks ago."

"Divorced? Already?" She frowned. "How old is she?"

"I don't know. In her early forties. Forty-five, maybe?"

Willow stared at me, her face carefully blank. "That's a big age difference, Ty."

I stared hard at her as the waitress set our orders on the table, silently asking her what the hell that had to do with anything.

"Don't look at me like that," she said once she'd thanked her, and we were alone again.

"It's like ten years. Tops." I picked up my fork. "And even if it's more, or less, who the hell cares? It's not like we're in high school. I don't see why it would matter at this point in our lives."

Willow took a bite of her food, but her attention was still focused on me. I felt her disapproval like a weight on my shoulders. And I totally didn't understand why it was there. I put my fork down without tasting anything, my appetite suddenly gone. Jesus Christ. I wasn't a fucking kid anymore. "What." The word came out harsher than I'd intended. I loved Willow like she was blood, but I was so tired of her mothering me. She'd done it our entire lives, and recently, it had gotten much more intense. I was a grown ass man, for God's sake.

"Don't be mad, Ty. I just worry about you. I want you to be happy. And this woman is just...I don't think she's for you."

"You've never even met her," I ground out. Why I was letting her get under my skin, I didn't know. But she was. My head was beginning to pound from this conversation.

"It's just that she's so much older than you. And divorced? You know there's gotta be baggage there. Does she have kids? How old are they? Is her ex-husband still around?"

I put my elbows on the table and rubbed my temples. "Fuck, Willow. I don't know. Where the hell is this coming from? All because I'm a little nervous over seeing a pretty woman again. This is ridiculous." I squeezed my eyes shut, trying to get my bearings as Willow droned on, her voice coming at me as though through a thick wall.

"Tyler? Tyler, look at me."

Her hand squeezed my arm. I concentrated on that feeling and tried to refocus. My heart was pounding. What the hell had just happened?

"Are you okay?"

I concentrated on her face, and gradually the roaring in my head eased up and all the little noises in the room became distinct again. The conversations of the other patrons, the soft clinking of silverware touching plates, the music playing from the ceiling, just loud enough to talk over. I looked down at the black tablecloth and was somewhat surprised to find myself still sitting there with my food untouched before me.

"Tyler? Are you with me?"

"Yeah, yeah." I rubbed my temples again. "Sorry, I don't know what happened there."

Her eyes traveled over my face, and then she smiled. "It's okay. It was my fault. I'm sorry. I didn't mean to upset you. Really."

"I know. It's okay."

She picked up her fork. "I really am sorry, Ty. I can tell you're stressed and I'm just adding to it. I wouldn't freak out about it."

Her calm demeanor washed over me. My stomach growled, and I followed her lead, digging into my food. "Yeah, I think you're right." Those days I'd lost not too long ago flashed through my mind, but I pushed it aside. It was probably just low blood sugar mixed with my temper rising or something. I'd be fine once I got some food in me.

CHAPTER 2

Ailee

$\mathcal{I}$ hit save and moved the photo I'd just finished editing into that model's file on my computer desktop just as the A/C kicked on in my little studio. With a sigh of relief, I turned my face to the cool—if a little stale-smelling—blast of air. Unfortunately, it did absolutely nothing at all to disperse the heat of the summer sun blazing through the old windows to my right.

For the third time in the last hour, I considered moving my desk from the front reception area to the back room, where the sun wouldn't beat down on me like a raging hot flash. But, like the other two times, I immediately discarded the idea as soon as I'd thought it. For one, there wasn't much room back there, as it was filled with all of my backdrops and props. Also, I only did shots out here if I wanted natural light. Which was next to never if I was shooting in the studio. And that was why I did all of my photography in the back room. If my desk was in there, too, I'd have no room whatsoever to maneuver and my hips would be forever covered in bruises from bashing into the heavy thing as I worked. Like most creatives, I would imagine, I tended to get lost in the view through my camera when I was shooting.

Besides, although the thought was nice now, in the middle of the hottest summer on record in western Washington, I really enjoyed sitting here by the windows the other nine months of the year. Even during the rainy winters.

Especially during the rainy winters. I loved the rain. There's a name for that. Pluvo...something. Pluvio-something? I can't remember.

And at least my meager A/C kept the sweat from trickling down my back.

Pluviophile! That's it.

Glancing through the open doorway that led into the studio portion of my little business, I thought back to the client I'd had this morning. The shoot today had gone really well, in spite of the rumors I'd heard about this girl. But whatever experiences other photographers had had with her, she'd been completely professional and pleasant in front of my lens, if a bit too young to be getting into this business.

Or, perhaps, I was just getting old.

I rubbed my forehead with the tips of my fingers in a vain effort to dispel the next thought, but it kept right on coming anyway...

In thirteen days, six hours, and four annnnd—I looked at the upper right-hand corner of my monitor—a half minutes, I'd be turning the big five-O.

Fifty.

Halfway to a hundred.

And for the first time in my life, I was beginning to feel it. And look it.

I had laugh lines appearing around my mouth and eyes. The skin on the back of my hands and eyelids was losing its elasticity. I was getting a double chin. My hair was more gray than brown (though I kept it professionally colored. Not quite ready to go *there*, yet). And my body, which I'd finally learned to accept somewhere in my mid-thirties, was beginning to sag in places my forever size eighteen figure had never sagged.

The only good part about being my age? Five years ago, after spending one week every month in excruciating pain for the last nine years, my doctors had finally come to the conclusion that I needed a full hysterectomy.

Best. Surgery. Ever.

I'm not even kidding.

Though it did leave a nice, long, horizontal scar across my belly, which sets off the vertical stretch marks my two children left there nicely. All in all, I didn't look twenty-something anymore. Or even thirty-something, for that matter.

And right up until this moment in time, I'd been pretty okay with that. But this upcoming birthday was hitting me hard.

Picking up my phone, I shook off the unpleasantness of my imminent leap into the next decade and checked the email that had just come in. It was from Stefanie Heathers, a romance author I'd worked with often, and someone I considered a very good friend. She needed some exclusive photos for one of her new covers, and per her usual mien, she had a model in mind. Perfect. That made my job a hundred percent easier. And it was one of the reasons I loved working with this particular author, who was also one of my best friends. Stef always knew exactly what she wanted, while also allowing me to have some creative rein.

I skimmed the email, picking up a few more details. She was going to be out of town for a few weeks for a signing/vacation, and she had already booked the model if I can squeeze them into my schedule—of course, I could—and the model she wanted was...

Tyler Hale.

My cheeks heated as my pulse picked up and a curious ache began to develop between my legs. I set my phone down and picked up the notebook lying next to my laptop, fanning my face as I tried to convince myself this was just a hot flash. Sweet Jesus. Just seeing his name was getting me all hot and bothered. I took a reinforcing lungful of oxygen. I was being silly, really. I'm a...mature woman, and fresh out of a fourteen-year marriage. And Tyler was probably, like, twenty-six, tops. A man who hadn't even hit his prime yet. He could be my kid, for God's sake.

I took another deep breath. I was being ridiculous, and unprofessional. Besides, what the hell would a guy like him see in me? I had tiger stripes on my drooping belly, my once firm jawline was disappearing into my neck, and my figure was rapidly descending into grandma territory.

Tyler, on the other hand, had a body as hard as a statue (I knew this because I accidentally walked into him at his last shoot) and probably hasn't aged a day since I'd met him a year ago.

Getting my head back into the game, I emailed Stefanie back and let her know what days and times I was available, which was pretty much whenever she would need me. Then I set my phone down and tried to ignore the fluttering in my stomach. No matter how my pre-menopausal hormones (thanks to the estrogen patches the doctor prescribed until I turned fifty-five) reacted to Tyler, I was a professional. I would handle this shoot—

Professionally.

I repeated this mantra to myself as I went about packing up my laptop and my camera for the walk home. Tyler had only been in front of my lens once before, and he'd nearly melted the damn thing. The man isn't even that good-looking, not like some of the guys I'd shot during my career. He's tall. And he obviously works out, of course. Dark hair and eyes, with a skin tone that led me to believe he may be of some type of Middle Eastern descent. All in all, on the good-looking but average side of the looks department. But he had a certain charisma that came through in photos, and practically smothered you up close and personal. Like...Antonio Banderas. Whenever I saw a photo of Antonio, I was just kind of like, "Eh." But I saw him once in real life when he was in town for a con or something, and I swear I would've fallen onto my knees and sucked him off right there in front of God and everybody if he'd so much as quirked a manicured finger in my general direction.

The effect Tyler Hale had on me was even worse. Muscled and tatted like the bad boy he probably was, he had eyes that pierced right through you. You know the kind I mean? Bedroom eyes. Eyes that looked at you and saw you naked. Hell, they singed the clothes from your body like lava.

I took another breath and focused on my laptop, opening up the file from yesterday's bridal shoot. Enough with the daydreaming about something I'll never have and don't need, anyway. I had work to get done. And these photos were going to take some major editing to come off looking the least bit like the happiest day of their lives.

Nothing like an angry bride to cool off my inappropriate libido.

THE NEXT TWO weeks flew by, and before I knew it, it was the day of Tyler's shoot. In spite of myself, I'd taken care that morning to look nice without looking like I'd tried to look nice. I wore my favorite jean shorts, an ombré purple T-shirt with a "V" neckline that showed off my cleavage, and my coolest pair of hip, slip-on sneakers.

Did people still say "hip"?

My mass of dark hair was artfully messy, and I'd spent an hour putting on makeup that made it appear I'd been born with this natural, youthful glow.

Tyler came in as I was in the back cleaning the lenses for my camera. I didn't even have to see or hear him to know he was there. My mating radar perked up as soon as he entered the reception area of my small, modest studio, the hair on the back of my neck standing up in awareness. A studio I was extremely proud of, by the way, because of everything I'd gone through to get to a place where I could afford the rent for a commercial space for my business.

And for the first time in my life, I'd done it all on my own, without any help from anyone.

I'd spent too many years being dependent on someone else, and for weeks after my divorce, I'd felt like I was standing on the edge of a cliff with my arms flailing wildly in the air, desperately trying not to fall into the dark abyss below even as my toes slid forward and rocks broke loose, the echo of them smashing against the side on their way down going on forever.

But now my feet were firmly planted on the earth, a safe thirty feet or more from that scary ledge. The strength it took to steady myself and back away had been there all along. I'd just been too wrapped up in my husband and kids to know I had it in me.

And now, after the hardest two years of my life, I'm in a place that's all about me. It sounds selfish, but I didn't care. And I was happy here.

He rapped lightly on the door to the back room where I kept my equipment and backdrops. It was where all of the magic happened. And where I was currently still hiding.

"Knock. Knock."

Chills chased each other up and down my arms at the sound of that deep, easygoing voice. Pasting a welcoming

—but professional—smile on my face, I set the lenses I was cleaning down on the table and turned to greet him.

"Hey, Tyler!" Too high! Too squeaky! Clearing my throat, I lowered my voice and asked, "How are you?" Sweet Jesus. He was even better looking now than he was the last time I'd seen him.

The Mediterranean god grinned. Not the sexy, knowing grin I'd seen him use in front of the camera, but an open and honest one. It lit up his features and completely took my breath away for a second. "Hey, Ailee."

My non-existent ovaries went into overdrive just hearing the way he pronounced my name.

"I'm good," he continued. "Just got done with my summer classes."

Oh, my God. I was lusting after a student. "Classes?" I repeated with that stupid smile pasted on my face. I tried to stop, I really did, but it was frozen there. Frozen. Like clown paint.

"Yeah, I'm going back to school and I needed to take some fillers." Crossing his arms over his muscular chest, he leaned against the doorframe. "It's been a while since I've done this sort of thing, but you know, I'm finding I appreciate it a lot more now than I did right out of high school."

Back to school. But how long had he been out? I tried to keep my eyes off his strong shoulders and biceps, displayed to my advantage by his pose and the white tank he was wearing. I failed miserably, so instead, I tried to make it look like I was only interested in what those arms were going to look like in front of my lens. "What are you taking?" Better. That sounded perfectly casual. Like I was only asking to make conversation.

"I'm starting law school."

His answer distracted me from his perfect arms. "Law school?"

"Yeah. I want to fight for people in the workplace with disabilities. Specifically, mental illnesses."

I didn't think it was possible to lust after this man more than I already did. I was completely and utterly wrong. "Wow. That's ambitious."

"It's something that's been on my mind for a long time. Of course, I may have to stop doing this." He looked past me to the area of the studio where I took photos. "I don't know that the courts would take me seriously after seeing me on the cover of a romance novel."

"That's too bad."

"Yeah, it really would be."

Something about his tone and the way he was looking at me gave me pause... But no, it was only my imagination. Wishful thinking. I gave myself an internal pinch. "Romance covers won't be nearly as attractive without you on them." As soon as I'd said it, I willed myself to disappear into one of the photos on the wall. "Uh, I mean..."

Luckily, he broke into my stuttering excuse for something cool to say. "It'll be too bad because I won't get to come here and see the way you look at me through that camera you love to hide behind so much." He opened his mouth like he was going to say more, but then he hesitated, his eyes uncertain for a moment before his features firmed into an expression of confidence. "I'd like to see you look at me like that without it."

Heat crept up my neck as he stared at me, and there was no mistaking his meaning this time as his eyes travelled slowly down my body. My pulse sped up so fast I got a little lightheaded and had to reach back and grip the edge of my desk to steady myself. The seam of my jean shorts between my legs was suddenly very noticeable, as was the soft lace of my bra scraping against my nipples when I took a steadying breath.

His nostrils flared, as though he could scent the change in my body chemistry on some primitive level. Dropping his arms to his sides, he took a step toward me. "Maybe we can still set up some private appointments. I could be available if you ever wanted to try any new techniques on me."

My eyebrows went up and my eyes glanced down at the bulge in his jeans, noticeably larger than it was when he'd first come in. My tongue shot out to wet my suddenly dry lips. There was really no mistaking what kind of techniques he was talking about.

The front door swung open behind him, and Stef came walking in with a young girl with big boobs, boyish hips, and long, straight, black hair. A girl Tyler's age. A girl with the freshness of youth all over her flawless face.

My pulse crashed back down to normal.

"Hey! What's going on, you guys?" Stef called out from the reception area as she set her stuff down.

I told myself not to panic. She always greeted me this way. But I couldn't stop the heat I knew was coloring my cheeks. I fanned myself with my hand and hoped she'd assume it was menopausal hormones.

Stef pulled the girl forward to meet me. "This is Cora. I found her last night at my son's house—she's a friend of his girlfriend—and I thought she'd be perfect with Tyler in this shoot, so I brought her along. I hope that's okay?"

Picking up my camera, I put the strap around my neck, looking anywhere but at Tyler, who still stood just inside the room, watching me intently. "Of course, hon. Anything you want."

"What about what I want?" Tyler asked quietly. His tone was teasing, but his dark eyes held a heated question when they met mine.

Cora spun around at the sound of his voice, and Stef shot him a grin.

He plastered that knowing, sexy grin on his face and turned to say hi to Stefanie and meet his partner for the shoot. The grin I now knew was totally fake.

Get it together, I scolded myself.

When Stef saw the two of them in the same room, she nearly squealed with delight. Running back over to me, she smacked my arm. "This is going to be so hot!"

I had to agree. The two of them looked great together with their dark hair and eyes. Tyler's skin was slightly darker than Cora's. Just enough to add some nice contrast.

After getting some last-minute thoughts on what she wanted for her cover, I shooed Stef back to a chair near the table behind me and had the two models stand together while I took some test shots. I adjusted the lighting, and then we were ready to shoot.

Tyler pulled off his tank as Cora stripped down to some sexy black underwear. I had to admit; the girl was gorgeous. A perfect partner for Tyler. I swallowed down the envy, stuck a smile on my face, and started directing them through some poses.

After about twenty minutes, I told Tyler and Cora to take a break while Stef and I perused the shots.

She shook her head. "I don't know why, but I'm just not seeing my cover."

They worked pretty well together, but I had to agree with Stefanie. The "it" shot just wasn't there. And I had a terrible feeling it was my fault. "I'm sorry. I'm just not on my game today."

Tilting her head, she studied the shots. "No. I don't think it's you. I think they just don't have the chemistry I was hoping for. Maybe if they don't look at each other?"

"Okay, let me see what I can do." Calling the two of them back, I did some profile shots with them facing each other with their eyes cast down. But it still just wasn't working. Peeking out from behind the camera, I asked Stef, "You said this is a *sexy* cover, right?"

"Oh, yeah." She grinned like she had a very naughty secret.

"Cora, would you stand in front of Tyler, please? No. Facing me." She turned around, so she faced the camera. "Right, like that. Okay. Tyler, stand behind her and put an arm around her waist, maybe with your hand on her hip." I lifted my camera to my eye. "Cora, don't look right at the camera."

I felt Stefanie come to stand behind me.

It still wasn't there. I thought at first it was Cora, that maybe she just wasn't comfortable in front of the camera. But she moved so naturally, with no shame whatsoever about her undressed state, that I was beginning to think it wasn't her at all. I tried to think of something that would add some tension to the shot. "Tyler, think of something you want and can't have, but you're determined to get."

Tyler slowly lifted his eyes and looked right at me, one side of his mouth turning up just a little as his fiery gaze burned right through my lens and into my most wicked fantasies. Slowly, he slid his hand up Cora's stomach until he cupped the underside of her breast, whispering something in her ear.

She smiled at the floor and nodded.

My breath hitched, and his eyes fell to my stiff nipples for just a second before they landed back on my face.

"Holy shit," Stefanie whispered. "That's it, Ailee. That's my cover!"

The camera shutter opened and closed rapidly as I took shot after shot. When it was done, I looked out from behind the lens and nodded at Tyler. He dropped his arm and stepped back, then started talking casually with Cora, keeping one eye on me.

Stefanie squeezed my arm. "You did it! We got it! I know it. Let me see."

I tore my eyes from Tyler's and guided Stef to the back of the room, where we looked through the shots. I had to admit she was right. This was the shot. "So, we're good?" I asked.

"Yup. We're good." She gave me a quick hug. "Thank you! Thank you! You're the best."

"Aww, I don't know about that. But thanks."

"No. Really. Thank you," she said. "I would ask if you wanted to grab some dinner, but I really need to get Cora back, so she's not late for work."

I barely held back my sigh of relief. "Don't worry about it. Another time."

Cora came over to thank me and to let me know she'd be open to doing more shoots. I got her contact info, and with a wave to Tyler, they were gone.

I stood there awkwardly with a lens cap in one hand, my camera in the other, and watched them leave. I should do something, but the weight of Tyler's stare, even from all the way across the room, made me self-conscious, and I couldn't bring myself to move. My emotions were all over the place, my body flushed one moment and trembling the next, and strangely, I felt tears burning my eyes. I just wasn't sure whether it was fear that all of his talk earlier had been one big hysterical joke...

Or, that he'd completely and utterly meant everything he'd said.

Then I laughed nervously to myself, and I might have even done it out loud. I couldn't tell you. All I could think about was Tyler seeing my naked body for the first time and abruptly changing his mind. I would be mortified. More than mortified. And what if word got around? Models talk, right? I had an excellent reputation as a photographer. I had that reputation because I always—

ALWAYS—remained pleasant and professional with my models, and because I listened to what my clients wanted. I was out of my mind to even think about messing that up.

But that wasn't the real reason I stood there staring longingly at the door through which there was no escape. The plain truth of the matter was this: I was way too old for this shit.

And yet a part of me...a newly awakened part of me... wanted nothing more than to feel Tyler's hands and mouth on my body.

CHAPTER 3

Tyler

"Are you going to look at me, Ailee?"

She shivered visibly at the sound of my voice, and that reaction, that proof that she wasn't as unaffected by me as she tried to make it seem, made the blood rush in my ears. Her blue eyes found me, then dropped to my bare chest, heating my skin before they alighted on the white tank crumpled in my hands. Then they wandered all the way down to my bare feet and back again. There was hunger in that gaze. No matter how she might try to deny it. Fucking hell. She made me weak with nothing but a look. I watched, entranced, as she put the lens cap back on her camera. Setting it carefully on the table behind her, she turned to me.

I studied her face, waiting for her to say something. Was I completely out of line here? I was coming on strong; I knew that. But this might be the last chance I'd have to see her since I planned to get out of the business, and I'd be busy with school again soon. It's not like I'd run into her on campus. Or find her on the bus. She didn't even live in the city, but out here, where the mist covered the mountains and the downtown area consisted of local business and the occasional rogue black bear.

Fuck, I don't know. Maybe I should get dressed, thank her, and head home. Save my dignity before she could turn me down. But I couldn't bring my limbs to move. I didn't want to get dressed. I wanted to help *her* get undressed.

She cleared her throat, the sound loud to my straining ears, even over the low music she'd put on while we worked. "It was a good shoot," she told me. "Sometimes, no matter how good a couple looks together, the chemistry just isn't there. We got the shot in the end, though, and Stefanie is happy. As soon as I get the edited copy to her and she pays me, I'll send you your cut."

Still trying to keep it to business only. I studied her face. Her skin was so smooth. So pretty. But her expression was almost desperate, her eyes pleading with me to play along. I didn't know why she was insisting on playing it so cool, but this was my chance—maybe my last and only chance—and I was taking it. If she shot me down, well, at least I wouldn't have to face her again.

And if she didn't...

I shook my head at her. "I don't give a fuck about the shoot." Tossing my tank to the side, I let my arms hang akimbo. "Come here." I threw the command out there. I couldn't just walk out of here without tasting her, without feeling her against me. Not without trying.

For a second, a flash of pure lust widened her eyes, only to be quickly hidden. It was so fast, I would've missed it if I'd looked away for even half a second. And when it was gone, instead of shock, or panic, a look of resignation swept across her features. "Tyler, we can't...this isn't..."

No. No more excuses. I saw the need on her face. The wanting. Just like I wanted her. If I let her, she'd talk us both out of this. "Ailee, come here," I demanded. My muscles hurt from forcing myself to stay where I was.

She glanced toward the door beside me that led out to the reception area. Hoping for an escape? But then she came back to me. Her posture straightened and her chin rose as she prepared to hold her ground. "Tyler, we can't do this. I can't do this."

"Why not?" I'm not exactly sure what had come over me. All I knew was I wouldn't—couldn't—allow her to pretend like this thing between us was something that happened every day. I'd felt it the first time I'd met her, but she'd had a wedding ring on her finger, and much as I'd wanted to, I wasn't about to pursue her when she had a family waiting at home.

But the ring was gone. The rumors were true. She had no one waiting for her now.

Ailee crossed her arms, and I recognized it for what it was —a protective gesture. My eyes fell to her breasts, spilling from the top of her shirt. Curling my fingers into fists, I forced my attention back to what she was saying.

"Because I'm..."

I took a step toward her, pulled by a force I couldn't fight anymore. "You're what?" Her lips parted as she watched me come toward her, but she didn't say anything to stop me. When I was within touching distance, I unclenched my hand and took her by the jaw, gently forcing her to look at me. I needed an answer—a good answer—as to why the hell we shouldn't be doing this. "Why not, Ailee?"

Her eyes got glassy with unshed tears. I didn't understand why she was so upset.

"Because I'm way too old for you, Tyler. And because I don't mix business with pleasure."

Too old? What the hell was she talking about? She sounded as bad as Willow.

And yet, a smile tugged at the corners of my mouth as relief rushed through me, making me lightheaded. Was that all this was about? A tear overflowed to dampen her cheek, and I brushed it away. "Ailee, don't you know what you do to me?" I forced her to look at me. "You wanna know why the shoot just now with Cora sucked? It was because I was trying so hard to distract myself from you that my head wasn't in the game. Not until that last shot. That last shot when I could look at *you*. When I could imagine being with *you*." Releasing her chin, I cupped her cheek in my hand and held her still so I could whisper in her ear, "I was so fucking hard she must've felt it, and probably thought it was for her. But this..." I breathed in the clean scent of her hair, "*thing* that I feel is completely for you."

She didn't seem to believe me, and I could think of only one way to prove my point. Needing to touch her, I ran my other hand down the bare skin of her arm, following a trail of goose bumps. When I reached her hand, I guided her to my aching cock. "Do you feel what you do to me, Ailee? I don't give a shit how old you are. You're sexy as hell. The sexiest woman I've ever met in my life."

I expected her to pull her hand away. Maybe give me a glare and a few choice words for daring to be so uncouth. Slap me even. It wouldn't be anything I didn't deserve. But though she stood stiff as a board, she didn't pull away, either. "Would you look at me? Please?" I waited, until finally, with agonizing slowness, she raised her eyes until they met mine. I said the only thing I could. The only thing that was true. "You take the breath from my lungs, Ailee." I leaned in closer, lowering my head so my eyes were at a level with hers. "I want you. So much I can't breathe. I've wanted you since the first time I saw you. And I think you feel the same way."

She leaned into me until I felt her soft breasts against my chest and her forehead resting on my shoulder. She took fast, shallow breaths. But still, she was silent, wouldn't admit to what I now knew was true. "What are you so afraid of, Ailee?"

The answer, when it came, made no sense to me.

"I'm afraid you won't like me."

What? How the hell could she think that after everything I'd just told her?

She continued to speak to my chest before I could argue with her. "I've had children, Tyler. I've had surgeries. Hell, I don't even have ovaries anymore. Or a uterus, for that matter. I'm..." She took a breath, and then cold air hit my bare skin as she stepped back, pulling away from me.

I held her hand, refusing to release her entirely.

"I'm fifty years old, Tyler. I get tired by 8PM. I like to stay home. My idea of a wild night out is meeting a friend for dinner and having a glass of wine. I'm not a young woman."

I never would've guessed she was fifty. She looked ten years younger. Yet it still made no difference to me. Age was just a number. It didn't change the fact that I physically ached for her to be in my life. I hadn't even realized how much I'd suppressed my need for her until the moment I walked in here today and saw her standing there. She was beautiful. Confident. Sexy. And not just her body. Her beauty shone from her eyes, her smile, her soul.

With a sniff, the woman I wanted more than anyone I'd ever met gave me a sad smile and pulled her hand from mine, turning her back on me.

I stared at the back of her head. She was dismissing me? Was that it? I started to turn away, but then I stopped. Ailee obviously thought she was making the right choice here, no matter how upset it was making her. But it was the *wrong* fucking choice. I knew it. And so did she. Even if she didn't want to admit it.

I took her by the arm and spun her back around to face me, sticking my face in hers until she had no choice but to look at me. If she thought something like a few stretch marks and a missing uterus was going to chase me away, she was about to find out how wrong she was. After all, I grew up with a sister, and a mother who didn't believe in hiding a woman's biology from the men in her life. "All of that just tells me that I can fuck you whenever I want without worrying about what time of the month it is. Although, I could've made that feel better, too."

Her eyes widened for a moment, and I could see her mind spinning, trying to think of another way to convince me what we had going on here was wrong.

Enough of this shit.

I kissed her. Not hard. Just a light touch of my lips to hers. But man, it was enough to send a sharp blade of lust into my groin. With a low groan, I increased the pressure, tasting her, exploring the softness of her mouth, getting the feel of her. Letting her grow used to me.

The urge to throw her back on the table behind her suddenly slammed through me, and I broke off the kiss, breathing hard. I stared at her, looking for signs that I'd gone too far, but not really caring if I had, and wondering where the hell that aggression had come from. Although, to be fair to myself, the action hadn't been to hurt her, just to have her.

Fuck me. I had to have her.

Wrapping her in my arms, I pulled her closer, her body fitting against me like it was meant to be there. She was breathing through her mouth, her swollen lips parted, her breasts pressing against me with each breath. I barely held back a groan of pure lust. "I want you, Ailee. So *fucking* much. Please...tell me you want me, too." My entire body began to shake in my efforts to hold still as I waited for her to tell me what I wanted to hear. To finally admit, she felt the same way I did. To tell me she wanted me, too. "*Tell* me, Ailee."

"I want you, too, Tyler. But—"

Fuck, no. No more "buts". I kissed her again, cutting her off and not trying in the slightest to hide my groan of pleasure. And this time, I didn't hold back. Ailee was mine. Even if she wasn't quite convinced of that, yet.

After a few seconds, she started kissing me back, her mouth just as hungry, pressing against me like she wanted to crawl inside my skin. I swallowed her moans, my hands trying to touch her everywhere at once. Even without my shirt on, I was burning up. I ached for her to touch me. Physically fucking ached. By the time she finally lifted her arms, sliding her hands up over my shoulders and then wrapping them around my neck, I thought I'd died and gone to heaven.

Her ass filled my hands and then some, and I squeezed the soft flesh before continuing my exploration. *Ah, God.* She felt even better than she looked. All curves and softness and heat.

I kissed her, my skin too tight and my body on fucking fire. I kissed her until I didn't know where she ended and I began. Every touch of her hands on my bare skin made me want to fall to my knees. And at the same time, I wanted nothing more than to force her to submit to me.

Shivers ran through me, my skin hot and cold. Thoughts filled my head, and I had no idea where they came from. Thoughts of sex and escape and anger screamed silently, chaotic voices shooting through the fog of rapture that already filled my head.

Desperate not to lose this connection with the woman I hadn't been able to get out of my head for the past year, I pulled up her shirt and slid my hands over her bare skin, sinking into the feel of her, rooting myself in her warm scent. I just wanted to slide into her and forget myself.

My head began to pound, and for a few seconds, I couldn't remember who I was or who I was with. Breaking off the kiss, I backed off, staring blankly at the woman in front of me.

Ailee. It was Ailee.

I repeated her name over and over to myself as it all came rushing back.

Voices screamed in my head from a distance, twisting in and out of each other until one voice—a male voice that sounded nothing like me—broke through the others.

Get out of here.

The room swam in and out of my vision and...this sounded completely fucked up even to me...but I felt myself separate from my body.

I struggled to focus. I tried to say her name.

Ailee.

Ailee was staring at me like I was some kind of freak.

I shook my head, trying to find some clarity. "I'm sorry, I have to go." The words came from my mouth, formed with the air in my lungs and the vibration of my vocal cords, but it wasn't me who said them.

And then there was nothing.

CHAPTER 4

Ailee

I checked my phone and silenced the incoming call, then slid it back into the pocket of my hoodie. Typical of western Washington summers, the warm temperatures from yesterday had dropped a good fifteen degrees today, and the evening was promising to be even cooler. Fall was definitely on its way.

"Who was that?" Stef grabbed my phone out of my pocket before I realized what she was doing. When she saw the number still lit up on the screen, she stopped dead in the middle of the sidewalk, forcing the other pedestrians to walk around us. "Tyler?" She frowned. "Is he asking about his money already? We just did the shoot yesterday, for fuck's sake. I haven't even seen the final edits yet." With a roll of her eyes and a toss of her head to get her dark hair out of her eyes, she slipped the phone back in my pocket.

I stood frozen to the spot in mortification. She didn't seem to notice.

"Why is he bugging you? Is he always this demanding?" She started walking again. "If so, I'm not using him anymore. No matter how freaking hot he is." She stopped in front of a little Thai place and looked at the menu in the window. "This looks good. Wanna eat here?"

I still stood in the same spot, my mind a complete blank as to what to tell her. Should I confess all of my dirty secrets? Let her confirm what I already knew about all of the reasons Tyler and I shouldn't be together? My phone started vibrating again. I didn't pull it out. I was afraid to look. Luckily, a pickup with a muffler of ridiculous proportions chose that moment to pass by us on its way down the narrow street, and it was too noisy for her to hear it.

Maybe she would move on to food and I wouldn't have to answer any questions. "Yeah, I've heard good things about this place," I told her in what I hoped was a casual tone. The odds were good I'd eaten there before—it wasn't like there was a large selection of restaurants in my small town—but for the life of me, I couldn't remember at this point in time. I forced my feet to move, grabbing the door from Stef as she went inside.

We ordered our food and some Thai teas from the counter and found a table by the window.

Two seconds later, I nearly choked on my drink when she said, "So, give me the details." Stef scooted her chair in and sat, looking at me expectantly.

I cleared my throat. "Details?"

"Yeah, on my edits. Is my cover going to be as awesome as I expect?" She grinned at me with dancing eyes.

The cover. Of course. "Um...yes. Yes," I said with more confidence. "That last shot was the winner. It's SO good, Stef. You're gonna love it." Of this, I had no doubts. And not because of our friendship. Stefanie never hesitated to call me out on anything she considered half-assed. Friends or not, she demanded the best, and I also knew what she liked and what she didn't. "I finished it up last night. After dinner, we can walk back to my place and I'll show you."

She clapped her hands with excitement one moment, then slammed them on the table the next. "I can't believe you're making me wait until after dinner."

I laughed. In my pocket, my phone buzzed, and I pulled it out without thinking about it. My smile fell as I saw Tyler's name on the screen. Maybe I should change his contact info to: Great Kisser But Kinda Stalkerish.

"Who the hell keeps calling you? If that's Tyler again, just answer it already." Stef thanked the waitress as she put our food on the table and picked up her fork. She looked up at me and must have seen something on my face. "What? What is it?"

I declined the call and set the phone down on the table. Thinking twice, I picked it up again and turned it off completely. I looked back at my friend, now chewing away on her Pad Thai. Stef's food waited for no one. "Stef, I almost had sex last night. Mind blowing, soul-altering sex."

Her eyes widened, and she swallowed. "With who?"

I took a deep breath. "Tyler."

She blinked once. Twice. "Tyler Hale? But he—"

"Is way too young for me. I know. God, I know. What the hell was I thinking?" I picked up my own fork and stuck it in the rice.

"I was gonna say 'has a girlfriend.' Why would you think he's too young for you?" Around another mouthful of food, she said, "And more importantly, what makes you think it would be soul-altering?"

I set my fork down again, choosing to ignore her second question. "Why? Because I'm fifty! And he's like...like...I don't know how old exactly, but he could probably be my kid!" I sat back, crossed my arms, and gave her an imploring look. "He has a girlfriend?" Of course, he did. Guys who looked like Tyler didn't ever *not* have a girlfriend. "So, I'm a child molester AND the other woman. Great." Suddenly, I'd lost my appetite.

"Well, there is a girl he's always hanging out with. I always assumed it was his girlfriend."

"Have you seen them together?" Stef, like me, was over the age of forty and single. Unlike me, she'd never been married. And also, unlike me, she still enjoyed going out to clubs. As she liked to remind me, "I'm forty-six. I'm not dead."

She dug into her food again and gave a small shrug. "Maybe once or twice."

"Recently?" I don't know why I wouldn't let this go.

She nodded as she chewed.

"And they were definitely together?" I pressed. "Like, *together* together?"

"Seems like it. I just saw them over the weekend. They were a ways ahead of me, but they were walking with their arms around each other and talking. I only spotted them because she has this really light blond hair."

At least she had the decency not to pity me. She looked more pissed at Tyler than anything. I took a deep breath. Okay, then. Last night was what it was. An ego boost from a young hottie that I really needed, and nothing else. I honestly hadn't known about the girlfriend, so I didn't need to feel guilty. Not if I cut off any more attempts from him.

Besides, why did he keep calling me if he has a girlfriend?

Stef's phone rang. I was grateful for the interruption in our conversation. I didn't want to talk about Tyler anymore. I'd turn my phone back on after Stef approved her cover photo and if he called again, I would set him straight for once and for all.

Unless, he was calling to tell me last night had been a huge mistake on his part. Maybe he'd taken something illegal, like ecstasy. That would explain his weird behavior. In that case, I'd crawl under the nearest rock and hide for the next twenty years. Or move to the other coast. Or maybe Europe. I've heard Italy is nice.

I looked up to find Stef waving at me with her free hand. "It's *him*," she mouthed.

I frantically shook my head, realized I was acting like a teenager, stopped, and then shook it twice as hard. I *was* acting like a teenager, but I just couldn't talk to him. Not yet. I hadn't had time to prepare what I wanted to say.

"Sorry, Tyler, I haven't seen her. But I'm supposed to stop over there in a little while and see the edits from the shoot, so I'll tell her you're trying to get a hold of her." She looked at me with wide eyes and shrugged. "Yeah, she probably just left her phone at the studio or something. She does that sometimes."

I shrugged back. This wasn't untrue.

She paused. "Yeah. Okay, I will...Okay...No problem... Good seeing you, too...You're very welcome...Talk to you soon." She disconnected the call and put the phone down on the table. "That was Tyler. He wants you to call him as soon as you can." Then she picked up a spring roll and dipped it in the bowl of sweet and sour sauce.

Don't ask. Don't ask. "Is that all he said?" Dammit. What was wrong with me?

She gave me a look. Not quite pity. More curiosity. "That's all he said. At least until you explain the 'soul-altering' part."

I snorted and went back to eating. "I'm going to call it off. Not that anything has really started. And you know exactly what I mean. I mean, have you met the guy?"

With a great sigh of disappointment, she said, "That's probably a good idea. And not because of the age thing. You're a young at heart, vibrant, attractive woman, Ailee. Hell, you're fucking hot. Any man would be lucky to have you. But you should call it off because of the girlfriend thing. If Tyler Hale wants to have you in his bed, he needs to break it off with Willowy Wanda."

I broke out into spastic laughter. "Willowy Wanda?" I said when I could breathe again. Good God. It wasn't that funny. Maybe I needed to have my estrogen levels checked. Have my hormone patch dosage adjusted.

She shrugged. "That's what I call her in my head. The girl is tall and so blond her hair is almost white. Not a curve to be seen. She reminds me of a willow branch. Or maybe a pussy willow." She stared past my shoulder with her forehead scrunched up in thought as she contemplated that one.

My heart sank in my chest. I was nothing at all like a willow branch. More like the tree trunk. Sturdy and planted firmly in the ground, with some pretty foliage when the mood struck me to do my hair and makeup. Maybe Tyler was just taking a wild ride on the chubby side last night. Maybe he has mommy issues.

I stared down at my food. I hadn't really thought about that. I guess it was totally possible.

"Ailee, stop. I can see the wheels turning. Whatever you're thinking about yourself right now isn't true. Tyler came on to you last night because you have an earthy beauty about you and he couldn't help himself. You're very sexy. Don't think I didn't see the way he stared at you while you were shooting."

"He was acting for the camera."

"He was fucking you with his eyes."

I laughed. I couldn't help it. Here we were, both middle-aged women, letting a boy dominate our conversation. "Let's talk about something else. Tell me about your book."

As Stef launched into an animated description of her characters and the awesome plot twist she'd come up with the night before, I ate my dinner and really tried to pay attention.

I swear I tried.

CHAPTER 5

Tyler

It'd happened again.

I woke up on the couch in my apartment. Snickers was sprawled out against my chest, and I was really glad for the shared body heat as I curled around him. For a few minutes, I dozed in and out of consciousness, until the vibration of my phone woke me.

Reaching beneath my ass, I frowned at the silky black boxers I was wearing. Did I even own a pair of silky boxers? Where the fuck had these come from?

I looked down at my phone. Willow. Tapping the screen to answer the call, I found the remote and turned down the television, where reruns of Mash were playing. "Hello?"

"Tyler?"

"Yeah. Who the hell else would be answering my phone?"

She sighed loudly. "Are you at home?"

Snickers squirmed over onto his back and sprawled out so I could rub his chest and belly. "Yeah, I'm at home."

"How'd the shoot go yesterday?"

Yesterday? I forced my brain to work. "Uh, good. It went good. I think Stefanie got the cover shot she was looking for."

"And how did things go with the photographer?"

Ailee...fuck! I struggled out from behind the dog and sat up. Goosebumps immediately broke out all over me. God, it was fucking cold in here.

I remembered telling her how I felt, and I remembered kissing her, but that was it. Everything after that was just...gone. I didn't even know how I'd gotten home. Apparently, I'd eaten, if the dirty dishes on the coffee table in front of me were any indication.

"Tyler?"

I scrubbed my face with one hand. "Fine. It was fine. What time did you say it was?"

"I didn't, but it's almost noon."

Not that long, then. I hadn't lost that much time. "Willow, let me let you go. I just woke up and I've gotta piss like a racehorse."

"TMI, dude. T-M-I. Call me later, okay?"

"Okay."

"Promise?"

What the hell was up with my sister? "Yeah. Yeah, I promise. I'll call you in an hour or two when I get up and around."

"Okay. Don't forget." And then she hung up the phone.

I set my phone down on the coffee table and wrapped my arms around my middle, trying to get warm. Then I tapped the screen and checked the date. It was noon the following day. Nothing worse than a hard night's sleep. Leaning forward, my stomach clenched in pain. It felt like it was full of rocks. Jesus Christ, what the hell had I eaten?

The thing was, I had no idea. I couldn't remember. I didn't even remember coming home. Had I taken the bus? Called a cab? Where the fuck was my wallet?

And how had I left Ailee yesterday? Was she all right?

I grabbed my phone and looked for her number. I knew I had it. I'd saved it last year when she'd called me for my address to send me my payment. But I'd just never had the balls to call her out of the blue and ask her out. When

I found it, I hit the green phone button. My mind scrambled for what to say. How to explain what had happened. And I had no fucking idea how to do that when I didn't know myself.

She didn't answer, so I left her a stilted message and put the phone down. I got up, trying hard to ignore the fact that I was on the fringe of a full-blown panic attack. My heart raced and cold sweat trickled down my spine, but somehow, I found some clean clothes and got in the shower. I hung my head, letting the scalding water loosen the muscles in the back of my neck. I didn't think about this latest blackout. Didn't wonder anymore about how I'd gotten home, or why this was even fucking happening to begin with. I didn't think about school, or the classes that were about to start, or if there was something really physically wrong with me, or if I was just going fucking crazy.

I didn't think about any of that shit. I let the water wash away the panic, and I took deep breaths, and concentrated on slowing my heart rate.

And I thought about Ailee. The curve of her cheek. The blue of her eyes. The shades of her dark hair and the way it fell in soft waves around her face. The tones of her voice. The way she moved with such understated confidence, comfortable in her skin. Sexy. Especially when she was behind the camera. The touch of her soft hands on my bare chest and shoulders...the feel of her lips moving beneath mine.

My heart sped up again, but for entirely different reasons, the main one of which was to provide blood supply to my stiffening cock. I lost myself in the fantasy, my hand sliding down my stomach to grip myself. I got off fast and hard, needing the release. When it was over, I stood there on weak legs while I caught my breath, and then soaped up my hair and scrubbed my scalp hard.

With pictures of Ailee dancing around the edges of my thoughts, I allowed myself to think about what had happened. I'd lost myself while I was kissing her. Like, fucking literally.

Something was wrong with me. I was no doctor, but I knew it wasn't normal to have blackouts like this. The first time it had happened, I'd blown it off, thinking it was from the alcohol. I'd been drinking the other times, too. Funny thing was, I never remembered making or ordering those drinks. Still, I'd attributed the bouts of amnesia to the alcohol. It wasn't unheard of. Maybe my body chemistry just didn't mix with hard liquor.

Yesterday, however, I hadn't touched a drop of alcohol. This I knew for a fact. I hadn't been drinking before the shoot. I never showed up for work under the influence. And I no longer kept alcohol in my house. Also, unlike the other times, I didn't smell it on my breath or sweating out my pores. Whatever nasty food I'd eaten, yeah. But booze? No. I was sure of it.

So, what the hell had happened?

My mind started racing again, imagining all kinds of reasons from an early onslaught of Alzheimer's to a brain tumor. Whatever it was, something was wrong with my head, that much was obvious. I couldn't ignore it anymore. I needed to go see a doctor.

A wave of panic seized me. I hated doctors. Hated hospitals even more. No one really knew why. I didn't know why, either. My foster parents, once they'd gotten me in their care, quickly discovered I had to be sedated for even the simplest checkups. And now, as an adult, I actively avoided anyone in a white coat.

The first years of my life, when I tried to remember them, are nothing but a burst of faces and noises and smells in my head. I remember the air being hot and dry. I remember a woman calling to me, her voice shrill with fear. And I remember loud noises, among a few other things. But these small memories all mix together in my head until it's like a bad movie or something. I stopped trying to remember shortly after finding my new family, and on my foster parent's advice, concentrated on forming new memories.

Once, I asked my new father where I'd come from. We were both in front of the kitchen sink, doing dishes after dinner. He'd put his hand on my head and told me it didn't matter. What mattered was that I was with them now.

Maybe they knew as much as I did.

I called Willow back. I didn't tell her about the blank spots in my memory, or about how worried I was that something was seriously wrong with me. I also didn't tell her about kissing Ailee. That was personal, between her and I. Willow had no place in what was happening between us. It was none of her business, really. She tried to get details, but I stuck to what had happened during the shoot and that was it. After a few tries, she gave up.

Then I tried to call Ailee again. Still no answer. I left another message.

I set about cleaning up the place, and then I took Snickers out to the park. Every once in a while, I'd try to call Ailee. By the fifth or sixth time, I realized she was avoiding me.

I needed to talk to her. To try to explain. I don't know what happened after I'd kissed her, but right now the only thing I gave a shit about was that she was okay. And the only way I would know that was if she would answer her fucking phone.

Back at my place, I got Snickers his dinner and tried one more time. It rang a bunch of times and went to voicemail. I threw some leftover pizza in the toaster oven and tried again. This time it went straight to voicemail without even ringing, which means she'd turned her phone off.

Fuck.

Fuck!

I paced the floor for a few minutes. Then I called Stefanie. She answered after the second ring. I asked her if she'd seen Ailee, and she said she hadn't, but that she was going over there after dinner. I asked her to tell her I'd called, and she promised she would. I thanked her and ended the call.

There was nothing else to do but wait. If I didn't hear from her tonight, I could always go by her studio tomorrow.

I was acting desperate. Fuck, I *was* desperate. The only thing that kept me from hopping on the bus and going to Ailee's place was the fact that Stefanie was going to be there to check out the edits from the shoot yesterday. I was desperate, but I wasn't some psycho. I didn't want to interrupt their business. Plus, I didn't know where she lived. Only that she'd mentioned once it was somewhere close by her studio.

I just had to trust that Stefanie would give her my message and hope that Ailee would call me back.

CHAPTER 6

Ailee

ater that night, after Stef and I checked out her cover shot and shared a glass of wine back at my apartment, I turned my cell back on.

Six missed calls. Holy hell, what had I gotten myself into?

Enough was enough. Without overthinking it—for once—I hit the call back button. He answered after the first ring.

"Ailee. Fucking finally."

He sounded so relieved, my red flags wavered and lowered to about half mast. Maybe something had happened. An emergency. An alien invasion, perhaps. "Hi, Tyler."

"I'm sorry for blowing up your phone. But I'd really like to see you. I need to see you."

The flags inched back up a foot or two. I took a deep breath and prepared myself to hold fast with my decision. "I don't think so, Tyler."

There was a long silence on the other line. "Ailee…"

"I just…this isn't going to work, Tyler. Besides, you have a girlfriend." This all came out in a hasty rush. I held my breath, waiting for his response. It was stupid of me, really, to hope he would tell me I was wrong. Whatever he said, whatever excuses he came up with, it wouldn't make a difference either way. It was just…his having a girlfriend would make all of this easier. I'm not that woman. As a rule, I don't date men who aren't available. Ever.

"I don't have a girlfriend, Ailee." His response was firm, but he didn't sound surprised that I'd said it. "Willow is my sister. We hang out. A lot. And people assume she's my girlfriend." He laughed. "Trust me, she's the farthest thing from it, but it comes in handy sometimes for people to think that."

My mouth dropped open. Her name was actually Willow? Wait until I tell Stef! But first, back to the current conversation. "It doesn't matter, really. That's not the reason I'm calling this off. Whatever this is."

"Ailee, I just want to see you. Tonight." He sounded frustrated. "Please. We can just get a beer." He paused. "Or maybe some coffee would be better."

I frowned at my empty wineglass. Why did I feel like I was missing something?

"Please, Ailee." He cleared his throat, and when he spoke again, his tone was assuredly lighter. "It's Friday night. Come hang out with me. Just for a while. And after the night is through and we've had a chance to talk, if you still don't want to see me again, I'll respect your decision. I swear."

Stay firm, girl. Stay firm. "I really can't. I have an early shoot tomorrow." Rolling my eyes at myself before I even uttered the words, I said, "How about tomorrow night?"

"Um, tomorrow might not work for me. I have a thing I'm supposed to do. Just...meet me at the coffee shop by your studio. I promise I'll have you home at a decent hour."

I was a masochist. That was the only explanation for the words about to come out of my mouth. "Fine. Okay. Give me thirty minutes."

"Great." I could hear the relief in his voice. "Thank you. I'll see you there."

After he hung up, I stood there staring at my phone. What the hell had I just agreed to? And what happened to all of the decisiveness I'd felt while talking to Stef? I groaned, then went to the bathroom to check my appearance. Coffee. That's all. Just coffee and conversation. He couldn't talk me out of my clothes in the middle of Maggie's Espresso.

Besides, he'd probably disappear again before anything could happen.

Tyler was waiting for me when I arrived thirty-five minutes later. He was staring at the empty chair on the other side of the table, one leg bouncing up and down as his fingers tapped a rapid staccato on the wooden top. He looked as nervous as I felt, but he stood and smiled when I walked up to the table, all of the tension leaving his body in a long exhale. And he was once again the cool, calm, and collected guy I was used to. "You're here."

"Hey, Tyler."

"Hey," he said softly. "What would you like to drink?"

"I can get it." I started to turn away, to walk to the counter. Or, perhaps, back out the door.

"No, please. Let me. I dragged you out of your house at this ungodly hour to come meet up with me. The least I can do is buy your coffee." His eyes twinkled with humor.

I caved. "A caramel latte with soymilk. Decaf, please."

"You got it."

I watched him swagger over to the counter. He was wearing jeans again, a little darker than the ones he'd had on last night, and a long-sleeved, dark red button-down shirt made of some kind of soft-looking material with a collar. Black sneakers were on his feet. With his dark hair and olive-toned skin, he looked like he'd walked straight off a fashion runway. The girl taking his order was young. Probably right out of high school. She laughed at something he'd said, her cheeks turning a bright pink as she peeked at him from under her lashes.

What am I doing?

I asked myself this for the hundredth time in the last half hour. Was it true Willow was his sister? What if she wasn't, and he was just playing me? Taking advantage of a lonely, older woman. I chewed on my thumbnail as I watched him chatting up the barista while he waited for my drink. Maybe this was all a big prank.

Or, maybe I just needed to chill out and enjoy the sex for however long it lasted.

Problem was, I knew me. And I didn't do casual sex. I'd tried once or twice in my life, and inevitably, I developed *feelings*. That was just the kind of person I was. I soaked in the energy around me and reacted accordingly. And I felt things pretty hard. This was why I'd veered far, far away from the dating scene ever since my divorce.

And there was no way in hell I wouldn't do the same thing with Tyler. Just from the few conversations we'd had over the last year since I met him, my instincts told me he was a genuinely nice guy. But nice or not, he was definitely the bad boy type. Intense. A little dark. The kind of guy I'd always found completely irresistible when I was young, and the kind of guy I normally stayed far, far away from now that I was older and had a little bit of sense in my head.

Last night was just...well, I didn't know what the hell had happened last night.

I scoffed at myself. His bad boy persona wasn't the real issue here. The real issue was that I was afraid. Say he really was available, and he really was that into me. My kids would laugh at me if I introduced them to this guy as their new...what? Mom's boyfriend? Stepdad?

My heart thumped as a sudden vision of Tyler, dark eyes intense with emotion, swearing himself to me and only me, flashed through my mind.

Blinking hard to break off *that* insane train of thought, I tore my gaze from his strong thighs—outlined so well in those jeans—and looked down at the table.

And then what? I grow older and fatter and more wrinkled while he remains frozen in time? Or practically. All of these curves he claimed to so love were hanging on to their youth by a thread. A very thin thread. One that was quickly unraveling.

People would think I was his sugar momma.

My friends and family would think the same thing when I introduced him as mine. All of them—except maybe

Stef—will call me a "cougar" and make fun of me like they do to the middle-aged men who date eighteen-year-olds. Instead of growing old gracefully with someone, I'll spend the remainder of my years fighting a losing battle with the aging process, all while trying to keep up with my beautiful, younger man. Spending all my money on Botox so his eye won't wander to the young baristas who are bound to stick their perky boobs in his face and promise him naughty things with big eyes weighed down by false eyelashes and not sagging skin.

"Ailee?"

I blinked to find that beautiful, younger man standing in front of me with a smile that hinted at nervousness, holding out a cup. His dark eyes travelled over my face, telling me things I really wasn't ready to hear.

I took the coffee from him, wrapping my fingers around the warmth. "Thank you."

Tyler sat down across from me. We stared awkwardly at each other for a minute. I didn't know what to say. I didn't know why I was here or what I was hoping would come out of this meeting.

Suddenly, he leaned forward, and his dark eyes pierced mine. A rush of warm heat raced through me and settled between my legs as the air between us became tense.

"I want to be with you, Ailee."

There was no doubt in my mind as to exactly what he meant by "be with you". I immediately shook my head, remembering how he'd walked out on me the day before. "I agreed to coffee, Tyler. That's it."

With a loud sigh, he leaned back. Fingertips tapped the table again as he studied me.

I sipped my coffee. Looked out the window. This was a mistake. I should just go home. Yeah. Home. I'll finish that bottle of wine Stef and I started and watch Netflix until I pass out. Worry about someone else's problems for a while.

On that note, I pushed my chair back.

He froze, panic coloring his features. "Where are you going?"

"Home." I gave him an apologetic smile as I grabbed my purse from the seat next to me. "Coming here was a mistake. This was a mistake." I started to get up.

He grabbed my hand before I could leave. "Please don't go. I'm sorry for being so blunt. I just...I don't know if I have much time."

A shaft of fear zipped through me. My knees gave out and my butt plopped back down on my chair. "What do you mean? Are you okay? Is something wrong with you?"

"No. No. Nothing like that. I mean, I'm not dying or anything. I just need to get home soon, too. And I'm not sure when I'll get to see you again." He squeezed my hand. "Please. Stay. Talk to me."

Against my better judgment, I slid the strap off my shoulder with my free hand and put my purse back on the chair next to me.

Hope spread across his handsome features. "Okay?"

"Okay." I could give him a few minutes. See what he had to say.

He settled back in his chair but didn't release my hand.

"Tyler, people are going to see us." People like his non-girlfriend. I glanced down meaningfully at our joined hands.

One side of his mouth turned up in a half-hearted smile. "I don't care if people see us, Ailee. I like you. I *more* than like you. And I'm good with the whole fucking world knowing about it. My only question is, why aren't you?"

"You left me yesterday." The thought that was at the forefront of my mind escaped before I could stop it.

He sobered. "I did?" He answered himself before I could. "I did. And I'm so sorry. I just...I don't know what happened. I wasn't feeling well."

"That's not what it felt like to me."

"What did it feel like to you?"

"Like you'd changed your mind. Like you suddenly didn't know what you were doing with me."

His eyes darkened as he leaned forward and dropped his voice. "That's not what happened, Ailee. I was there. With you. I was totally in it. I swear this to you."

I hated exposing myself like this, but I had to know. "Then why did you leave like you did? We were kissing and then we weren't. And you were running out the door."

His eyes burned into mine. "Ailee, I'm sorry. I'm so sorry. It wasn't you. I swear it wasn't you."

Did I believe him? I didn't know. "Tyler, what exactly are you hoping to get out of this?"

He frowned. "What do you mean? Like, what are my intentions toward you?" He grinned, lightening the mood. "Do I need to go speak with your father? Get his permission to court you?"

I felt like an idiot. "Well, yeah. I mean no. Kind of. What I meant was, is this just a fling until you get whatever this is between us out of your system?"

Reaching across the table with his other hand, he covered my fingers with both of his and looked me right in the eye. "No, Ailee. This is much more than just a fling for me."

My heart began to pound in my chest. "What is it, then?"

"I can't really answer that question just yet. I can't see into the future. But I *can* tell you, I feel things for you, Ailee. Strong things. Scary things." He laughed quietly, the sound so sexy I could listen to it all night. "You know, the first time we worked together, I could barely spit out my name when you shook my hand. You were so confident and poised and professional. And stunningly beautiful." He smiled at my look of disbelief. "A little distant." Looking down at our joined hands, he rubbed his thumb back and forth across the back of my knuckles. "Yet there was something that danced in your eyes that I really wanted to find out more about." He pinned me in place with his stare. "I couldn't stop thinking about you. I haven't stopped thinking about you since that day. You weren't available then." He rubbed my ring finger, now devoid of any kind of jewelry. "But you are now. I wasn't sure if the rumor was true until I saw you again. And I knew, right then, that I couldn't let this lovely lady with so much life in her eyes get away again. Not without a fight."

"Are you sure it's not cataracts you're seeing?" But my self-imposed joke fell flat.

The last trace of his smile fell from his face, and he frowned. "Why do you do that?"

I raised my eyebrows and pulled my hand from his. "Because it's the truth, Tyler. I told you how old I am."

He let me go this time, his hand clenching into a fist before dropping beneath the table. "Ailee, you *still* don't fucking get it. I don't *care* how old you are. It's just a number. It's not you."

I pressed my lips together to stop myself from saying more.

"You're worrying about a future that hasn't even happened yet." He sighed heavily. Leaned forward again. "Look. Just...agree to date me."

I crossed my arms. "Date you."

"Yeah. You know, dinners, movies, romantic strolls in the rain." A devilish light in his eyes chased away the shadows from my comment. He was probably thinking about wet T-shirts. "Breakfast in bed." He paused, searching my face. "See what happens and take it from there."

I wracked my brain for more reasons why this shouldn't happen. But it was impossible to think straight when he was being like this.

Leaning back, he opened his arms wide. "What can I tell you that'll convince you I'm worth it? Ask me anything, and I swear I'll give you an honest answer." He gave me a devilish grin.

"Okay," I told him. "Why did you run out the door yesterday? The truth this time."

The smile slipped from his face. He took a sip of his coffee, and wouldn't meet my eyes.

My heart began to race and suddenly the familiar smells I usually found so comforting overwhelmed me until I felt nauseous. The murmured conversations around us became a rush of sound in my ears. "You just told me it wasn't me."

"It's not." His answer was short, the words clipped.

I had to admit, part of me was ready to call it. To thank him for the coffee and walk out the door. But another part of me—that part of me who craved drama and excitement and always used to go after the bad boys—kept me in my seat to see what else he had to say. To figure out the mystery that was Tyler.

He chewed his lower lip and stared down at his coffee cup. Both hands were wrapped around it, and he tapped one side on the table in a steady rhythm. Every few seconds, he would glance up at me, then back at his cup.

I let him stew on whatever he was thinking, until finally, he rubbed his eyes with the fingertips of both hands and sat back in his chair. "I need to tell you something about me. I was hoping I could give you a chance to get to know me better first, but I don't think I can put it off or I'll end up lying to you to cover up my actions, and I don't want to lie to you, Ailee."

Wow. I didn't know what to say to that, but my curiosity was definitely peaked. Still... "You don't have to tell me anything you don't want to, Tyler."

He rubbed his eyes again. "Yeah. Yeah, I do."

I took a sip of my coffee, trying not to cough when I forgot to blow on it, and waited to hear whatever it was that was so distressing. My mind started spinning, imagining all kinds of scenarios, but nothing I imagined could prepare me for what he eventually told me.

CHAPTER 7

Tyler

"I do not have a girlfriend," I told her. And that was the truth. In high school, I'd dated a girl for about six months, and that was the closest I'd ever gotten to having a long-term girlfriend. I loved women, but when I was in college, I was too worried about my classes and too tired from studying to put in the effort for anything beyond casual dating. And when I needed a feminine ear to listen to me, my sister had always been there. "The only other woman I hang out with is my sister. She's an important part of my life. Sort of like...an emotional support person."

Ailee laughed. "You're comparing your sister to a dog?"

The sound of her laughter warmed my heart, even if I was the brunt of the joke. "Not all emotional support animals are dogs. Some are cats. Or rodents. I saw one guy with a peacock once." I couldn't help it. I grinned.

One eyebrow lifted, and she gave me her "don't bullshit me" face.

I tried not to laugh. "I'm dead serious." She still didn't seem to believe me, but she let the peacock comment go. "No, but really, she watches out for me. I'd really love for you to meet her."

"So, what's the big, terrible thing you have to tell me?"

"What makes you think it's bad?"

"If it wasn't, you would've told me by now. And the fact that you haven't is making me kinda nervous."

I leaned forward, forcing her to look at me. "I'm not a serial killer or anything, Ailee. Nothing like that."

"Drug addict? Alcoholic? Felon?"

I shook my head. "No. At least, not that I know of."

Again with the eyebrow. "That you know of?"

How to tell her what was going on without sounding like I just escaped from a mental institution? Or that I needed to be in one? I took a sip of my coffee, stalling for time. Maybe it was too soon. I didn't even know myself what the hell was going on with me, and the last thing I wanted to do was scare her off. Not when I finally had a chance to be with her.

Besides, what the fuck was I going to say? *Oh, by the way, if I ever happen to not call when I say I'm going to or I stand you up or something it's not because I'm a douche, it's just that I've been having these episodes where I completely black out and wake up behind trash cans, stinking of whiskey and women I may or may not have fucked because I can't remember...*The thought sobered me. Shit. I needed to go get tested for STDs.

"Tyler? What is it?" Her voice was hushed, concerned.

I was worrying her, and that was the last thing I wanted. My mind spun. Now that I'd opened this can of worms, I needed to tell her something. Anything.

Maybe not everything.

I put down my cup. "Ailee, I've got something going on. Some...health stuff." I raised my hand at her look of alarm and shook my head. "It's nothing serious." I hoped. "But I just wanted you to know about it in case you hear anything." Like if I end up in jail.

"What kind of 'health stuff'?" Almost immediately, she waved away her question. "Never mind. It's none of my business."

I grabbed her hand from the air and pulled it toward me. "It is your business. I want it to be your business. I want everything about me to be your business." She tried to pull her hand from my grip, and I let her go, wrapping my own back around my cup to replace the warmth she'd just stolen from me. "It's..." I paused. "I'm not exactly sure what's going on with me yet. I have a doctor's appointment set up. I've just been having some episodes." I laughed self-consciously. "I don't know how to explain it without making me sound like one of those people you see on TV. All I know is leaving my house probably isn't the greatest idea these days."

"Like Agoraphobia? You have anxiety issues?" She frowned. "Though that doesn't really make sense if you're sitting here in public with me."

I exhaled, frustration twisting my insides and sharpening my movements as I sat back in my chair. A flash of pain tore at my skull and I took another breath as I rubbed my temples for a few seconds. "Look, there's more to it than that. I think maybe I had some hard stuff in my life, or something. I don't really remember. And it might be causing some issues." I dropped my hands back down to my cup. "But it's not something I want to share right now. Is that okay? I just wanted to let you know that something is up with me, and it has nothing at all to do with you or what's happening between us."

She stared at me hard for a few seconds, and I wished so much that I could read what was going on in her head. "So, Willow is your support person."

"Willow is my sister. My older sister. Not blood, but we grew up together in the same foster home. She still thinks she needs to take care of me."

Ailee gave me a strange little smile, then stared down into her cup. "I don't know, Tyler. I don't know if I can be one of those women."

What the hell was she talking about. "What kind of women are those?"

"I'm not a mother figure who's going to take care of you. And I'm not the kind of person that comes between another woman and the man she loves."

Was I missing something here? "Didn't you hear what I said? Willow is my sister, Ailee. There's nothing like that between us."

"That's not what I hear from people who've seen you two together."

People needed to mind their own goddamned business. "You're wrong, Ailee." God, this was almost funny. "Willow is my sister—"

"Not by blood."

"No, but—"

"Thank you for the coffee, Tyler. But last night... shouldn't have happened. It was wonderful. Really, it was. But it shouldn't have happened. So, let's leave it at that and walk away as friends. Okay?" She stuck out her hand.

I glanced down at it but made no move to shake it. "I wish you would reconsider."

"I don't think I will." She pulled her arm back and gathered her things. "I don't have time for these kinds of complications in my life."

So, now I was a complication?

Fuck. I shouldn't have told her anything.

"But I wish you the best. Really. And thank you for reminding me there are other things in life besides work." Her blue eyes shone with sincerity.

She really didn't know how alluring she was. I crossed my arms over my chest. Her blasé attitude was beginning to piss me off. "If you're about to throw cash at me for services provided, please don't. I never finished the job."

She froze, her eyes flying to my face. "That's not what I'm trying to say here."

"I know." I scrubbed my face with my hands. I wasn't being fair to her. She had every right to be cautious. She didn't know me. Not well, anyway. She wasn't being unreasonable. She was being smart. Much as I hated to admit it.

Before I could say anything else, she turned and started walking out the door. As I watched her retreating figure, my chest felt like it was caving in on itself. My head told me to let her go. But every other part of me told me to stop her. I decided to listen to *that* part. I couldn't let her walk out of my life. I just couldn't.

"Ailee, wait!" I caught up to her before she could escape into the night. "At least let me walk you home."

"That's really not necessary." She walked out the door.

I followed her, gently grabbing her arm before she could get too far away. "Please, Ailee. I swear I'm not trying to be creepy. I just want to make sure you get home safe."

"It's a small town, Tyler."

"Strange things happen in small towns, too."

She stared up at me, and I tried my best to hide the desperation I felt to keep her near me.

"All right. But you're not coming up." She pointed her finger in my face and used her best "mom" tone on me. It didn't scare me. I'd heard that tone before from my actual mom. It had no effect back then, and it had no effect now.

My smile held a hint of triumph. I knew it, but the best I could do was keep it out of my voice when I told her, "I would never be so presumptuous."

Somehow, I don't think she believed me.

We started walking, neither of us in any great hurry. "Thank you again for the coffee," she said.

I looked down at her. I couldn't just never see her again. I searched the dark street for inspiration, but saw nothing but wet roads, trees lining the sidewalk that showed the first hints of fall, and the occasional pedestrian. It was getting pretty cold, and I wanted to pull her in close to me, but I knew physical closeness wasn't what would ultimately convince her to give me a chance.

Play it cool, Ty. "Where did you grow up? Around here?"

She glanced over at me as I walked casually beside her, hands shoved deep in my front pockets. I lifted an eyebrow as I waited for her response.

"Um. In the northeast."

I waited for her to say more. She didn't. "In a city?"

"Uh, no, actually. It was a small town. Smaller than this one."

"So, you grew up in the country."

She shrugged.

I'd been to New York state once. It was beautiful. "Did you have a farm?"

She laughed. "No. We did not have a farm. Although we did have chickens. And a few turkeys." She took a deep breath, raising her face into the cool, damp night air. "I miss the stillness," she told me suddenly. "The sound of the rain and the rustle of the trees. I like listening to the crickets sing and waking up to herds of deer in my yard."

"Where you grew up?"

"Yes. But also here. That's why I moved out here from the city."

"Because it reminds you of where you grew up." I could smell the rain that was coming and the crisp scent of fall. A lot different from the air in the city.

"Yeah. It kinda does. Just everything's bigger here. The mountains. The trees." She cleared her throat, and I felt her retreat into herself for a moment before she came back to me. Chasing away memories of days long gone and people that weren't ever coming back. I knew that feeling.

"What about you? Where did you grow up?"

"In Texas, mostly. My foster parents still live there."

She stopped walking. "I didn't realize. You said Willow was your foster sister, but I assumed she was the only one who was fostered."

"Most people don't."

"You weren't adopted?"

"Neither of us was adopted. Not that our parents didn't want to, but they had their reasons." Or, so I'd always assumed. All I knew was that they loved us like we were their own. And that was good enough for me. I reached for her hand, and she let me take it as we began to walk again. "Willow was already placed when I came along. We were both really young. According to our parents, she took to me right away, taking on the big sister role like she'd just been waiting for me."

She had questions. I could tell by her silence and the funny look on her face every time she glanced my way. I gave her a small smile to let her know I was open to answering whatever she wanted to know, but she kept her thoughts to herself.

The wind kicked up, blowing her hair around her head. She brushed it out of her face with her free hand, a bit awkwardly, and a small thrill went through me that she was unwilling to make me release the hold I had on her other hand. She squeezed my fingers as we walked past the small restaurants and business that lined the main street. Offering me sympathy?

When we reached the end of the street, we turned left, and she pointed out her apartment building. I could see it through the mist, about three blocks away, maybe less. I was running out of time. "I don't know much about where I came from, except I was born somewhere in the Middle East and I wasn't an easy kid when my foster parents, Jim and Elaine Hale, got me. Apparently, within a year, I'd already been in and out of three other foster homes before them. They gave me a family, and probably kept me from trading life in the foster system to life in the prison system. And when I was old enough, I had my last name legally changed." Saying it out loud left me feeling exposed. I wasn't sure why. I was more grateful to my parents than they would ever know. The love I felt for them knew no bounds.

"Probably?"

I laughed a little. "Most definitely. I like to think I would've taken the necessary steps to straighten out my life on my own, but honestly, I don't know what would've happened to me if they hadn't come into my life."

"But you said you were young when you went to them."

"I was, but that doesn't mean I was easy. Apparently, I'd been through some trauma the first years of my life." I shrugged. "I don't know. I don't remember much."

We walked in comfortable silence until we reached the door to her apartment building. I wanted to keep talking, but it was also nice to just be with someone, without having to be "on" all of the time.

All of the units were inside for security reasons, although I couldn't tell you what the builders thought they were protecting their tenants from, despite my words from earlier. Bears, maybe?

She released my hand and smiled at me.

Okay. This was it. My last chance. "Look. I heard what you said back at the coffee shop. I did. Really. But, just think about it, Ailee. Please? A date or two. That's all I'm asking. Dinner."

"Tyler—"

"It's just dinner," I told her. "No expectations. Just..." I caught her eyes with mine, "give me a chance here, will ya?"

She gave me a look like she didn't believe me.

"I didn't say I wouldn't be hopeful." I grinned at her, my body warming at the memory of her in my arms. "But I won't push it...much."

To my relief, she laughed. "We'll see."

Did that mean what I thought it meant? "So, yes?"

After a slight pause, she nodded.

I sucked in a great lungful of oxygen. I didn't think I'd taken a full breath since we'd left the coffee shop, but at her answer, I felt like I was about to float away. I didn't know what made her change her mind, but I'd take it. "Great! Awesome. I'll call you. Okay?"

She tried to smile. It faltered a little at first, before widening into something that was true. "Okay. Fine. Dinner. That's it."

The rain started to fall again, a little more in earnest this time, so I cupped either side of her face and dropped a kiss on her soft cheek. "I'll talk to you soon."

She stared at me for a few seconds, nodded, turned, and walked slowly into the building. Inside, she glanced back through the glass. Her lips parted when her eyes landed on me, and I could only imagine the raw need she must have seen on my face. It was a risk, showing her the anguish I felt in my soul. I should have schooled my features. Hid this worrisome need I had for her. But I didn't. I let her see it.

She stared at me, her chest rising and falling with her quick breathing, before she pressed her lips together into a tight smile, giving me a little wave before she turned on her heel and strode away.

I returned the wave, though she didn't see me, and waited until she was out of sight before I made my way to the bus stop to catch my ride home.

Halfway there, the world went woozy and pain lanced through my temples. My vision faded in and out, and I stuck out a hand, looking for something to steady myself.

Fuck.

Fuck!

CHAPTER 8

Ailee

Four days had gone by and I hadn't heard a word from Tyler. In that time, I'd kept myself busy with work, checked in with the kiddos, and most definitely did not think about why a man who had stared after me with such raw lust hardening his features wouldn't have called yet.

But Lord help me, I could still feel his eyes burning all the way down to places I didn't even realize I had the night he'd walked me home. Somehow, I'd kept my steps steady and measured as I'd walked away from the door, refusing to look back again or over-analyze what I'd agreed to.

That moment he'd dropped his guard, though. That look. It still made my knees weak.

Had any man ever looked at me like that? Like he would rip off doors and tear down walls to get to me if I so much as quirked a finger in invitation? I had to admit, I couldn't think of one. Sure as hell not my ex-husband. Once he'd gotten me to the altar, I'd been lucky if he'd even noticed me walking into the room. And after I'd gotten pregnant the first time, we may as well have had separate bedrooms. The second time had happened after too much alcohol at his office Christmas party.

The way Tyler looked at me was kinda scary, a bit obsessive...and yet, it sent a thrill through me. I mean, what woman wouldn't want a man to look at her like that?

But at the time, I'd closed the apartment door behind me, turned the deadbolt, and set my purse down on the table in the foyer. Then I'd wandered into the kitchen on autopilot, where I'd poured a glass of water and leaned back against the counter. I wondered how long he'd stood out there, and I had to admit, it had crossed my mind to have a change of heart and invite him inside, knowing damn well what would've happened if I had.

What I'd told Stef was no lie. If the way he kissed was anything to go on, having that man in my bed would, in fact, be a life-altering experience.

But in the end, I'd set my empty glass in the sink and turned off the lights before making my way into my bedroom, where my vibrator and I had had one hell of a bonding experience.

"Why don't you just call him, Ailee?" Stef grabbed a slinky, deep red piece of material from the rack, pulling me back to the here and now. "And you could wear this when you see him!"

I willed away the vision of Tyler's burning eyes. Shopping. We were shopping. "Is that supposed to be a shirt?"

She rolled her eyes. "It's a dress. And it would look amazing on you."

The woman was insane. I refused to take the "dress" and went back to my retail therapy. I actually wasn't big on shopping, but when Stef called and asked me if I wanted to get together for lunch and to help her pick out a dress for some mysterious occasion she wouldn't elaborate on, I'd jumped at the chance to head to Seattle. I needed the change in scenery. And it was, most definitely, not in the hope that I would run into Tyler. That was just silly. There were a lot of people in the city. The chances of running into anyone you knew were pretty miniscule.

That was absolutely not the reason.

While we shopped, I'd filled her in on our coffee date. And now she was way too excited about a date that may or may not happen and that she wouldn't be going on anyway. "For one. No, it wouldn't. And two. It's too cold and wet to wear something like that anywhere outside of the dressing room."

"So, wear a raincoat."

"Stef, be serious."

"I am being serious. Any man would take one look at you in this and would have it off of you within six seconds, guaranteed."

"Then what's the point of wearing it?"

"That is the point. That's the only point."

It was my turn to roll my eyes. I found a navy cocktail dress with a halter neckline and a pretty design of crystals covering the bodice. "What about this one for you? Too fancy? Not fancy enough?"

Her eyes lit up when she saw it. "Ooh! Pretty. Add it to the pile."

Forty minutes later, we left the store. Stef had a bag with her new dress draped over her arm—the navy one—and we were both ready for lunch. (Because you didn't eat before you try on clothes. It's just a rule. All women knew this.)

Luckily, the rain we'd been promised that day was still holding off, but I pulled up the hood of my jacket as we came to the crosswalk, just in case. Glancing at the infamous Space Needle, I couldn't help feeling a little bit like I was in the middle of Grey's Anatomy. The light turned, and I dropped my eyes.

Just in time to see Tyler walking straight toward us.

I jabbed Stef in the ribs as we began to cross.

"Ow. What?" She frowned at me.

I widened my eyes at her and flicked them toward the man briskly walking toward us. His head was down against the wind, arms pulled in tight against his sides, eyes on where he was walking, and I wasn't sure what to do. I couldn't very well stop him in the middle of a busy intersection.

"Hey, Tyler!" Stef took the decision out of my hands. "Just act natural," she muttered from the side of her mouth.

Tyler kept walking. He didn't even look up.

She called him again when he was only about five feet from us. He didn't respond, just walked past without so much as a glance. I grabbed her arm and pulled her the rest of the way across the street. We both stopped and turned, watching him walk away.

"Was he wearing ear buds or something?" Stef asked.

I tried to hide the hurt I was feeling. "Not that I saw."

"Well, then what the hell?"

"Maybe he was just deep in thought, and with all the construction and cars and people—"

Stef cut off my words with a look. "Don't make excuses for him. That was a complete douchebag move."

I turned away from the sight of his retreating form. "Yeah. It kinda was."

We exchanged the same "fuck him" look, and continued on to the restaurant, a little place we both loved that served just about anything you could think of in a wrap.

Much as I hated to admit it, Tyler's snub had hurt more than it should. And as much as I tried to defend his actions to myself—there were so many people and cars and buses and maybe he had those cordless earbuds in or something—the truth was it hurt that he hadn't been aware of me. Like, at all. I mean, both Stef and I had been right in front of him. She'd practically blocked his path in the middle of the intersection, and he'd sidestepped her without even glancing up.

Yummy smells, bustling wait staff, and the clink of silverware accosted me as we entered the restaurant and my stomach growled in accord, distracting me from my troubles. Grabbing a table in the corner, we both ordered tea and a vegetarian wrap. Once the waitress had left, I pushed Tyler from my mind and tried to get more information out of Stef about our mysterious shopping trip.

"So, come on. You're not seriously gonna keep holding out on me about the dress after I was publicly dumped in the middle of downtown Seattle."

She grinned as the waitress returned and set our teas down. "You weren't dumped. You were ignored. Besides, how could you be dumped? You're not even dating." She took a sip of her tea. "Yet."

"Try 'never' if today is any indication."

Stef looked past me, her forehead screwed up in deep thought. "Maybe we should give him the benefit of the doubt, 'lee. I've never known Tyler to be an asshole."

"Until today."

"Maybe he had a good reason to be so obtuse. Maybe his mom is sick or something."

I pulled my own tea toward me and took a sip. "He's adopted. Well, fostered. Did you know that? Spent a year in foster homes until one family finally kept him."

"No shit." Stefanie obviously didn't know this piece of history about her favorite model. "I just don't understand how a mother could give up a child, unless it's under extenuating circumstances." I could see her imagination running wild as her inner author took over. "Makes me wonder why his birth mom made that choice."

"Me too, but I didn't ask. And he told me he didn't really know much about where he came from. Only that he was born somewhere in the Middle East."

"That would explain his gorgeous skin and smoldering dark eyes."

Even though I'd had that same thought myself more than a few times, I had to laugh. "Smoldering?"

"Girl, you know they smolder. It's hard to hold it together watching him pose for the camera. I don't know how he does it." She paused and looked away, her face scrunched up in deep thought. "Oh, wait. Yes, I do. It's because he's looking at you, the woman he's lusting for who won't give it up."

Our meals arrived, and we temporarily put our conversation on hold while we shoveled it in as fast as we could. Stef and I both had no shame in our eating game. It was one of the reasons why we were such good friends. When I felt like my stomach wasn't touching my backbone anymore, I took a drink and stared at Stef with my fork hovering over my food. "You really think I'm being stupid for making such a big deal out of this whole age thing?"

"Yes," she told me without hesitation. Then she grabbed a French fry.

I set down what was left of my wrap and brushed my hands together, my appetite suddenly gone. "Don't beat around the bush, Stef. Tell me how you really feel."

The waitress came over to check on us, saving me from whatever smartass remark she was about to make. "This is all a moot point," I told her when she left again. "You saw him. Not thirty minutes ago, he completely ignored me. I mean, I practically brushed shoulders with him. There's no way he didn't see us. And," I continued when she opened her mouth to put in her two cents. "I haven't heard a word from him in almost a week. Not a text. Not a quick phone call. A dick pic. Nothing."

"Would you really want a dick pic?"

"Of course not. That's not the point."

"What is the point?"

I released an exasperated breath. "The point is that I'm way too old and entirely too busy to be sitting here wasting our entire lunch doing guesswork about a guy like we're still fifteen or something."

"Then why do you keep bringing him up?" Her expression was completely serious, but her eyes danced with humor.

I laughed. "Stop it. And I'm not bringing him up anymore. I'm going back to my life as usual." I eyed her as I took a sip of my tea. It was time to turn the tables. My friend was hiding something from me. And for a woman who was usually an open book, it must be something juicy. "So! Who's your hot date?"

Caught off guard, she choked on her food. Watery eyes looked up at me as she reached for her tea. I waited patiently while she took a drink and bought time to think up a good reason that I was pretty positive would have nothing at all to do with the real reason.

"It's just a work thing."

A work thing? She was an author. Most of the time she was holed up in her house in sweatpants and a stained T-shirt with her hair held back off her face by her headphones. "Like an office party?" I teased.

Stef leaned back in her chair and patted her full stomach. "I wouldn't wear rhinestones to an office party. Even if I had an office."

"Come on, Stef. Give it up. I've told you all my secrets." I normally wasn't this nosey, but I really needed something to take my mind off my own issues. "Spill."

She gave me a shrug. "It's really no big deal. I entered two of my books for an award and I needed something pretty. Just in case I win."

I didn't buy it. The only award ceremony I'd heard her say was worth entering took place during the summer, which meant there wouldn't be another one until next year. Why would she be buying a dress for an event so far away? Anyone who had weight fluctuations—aka most women—knew better than to do that. "That's your story?"

"Yup. And I'm sticking to it." She grinned as she waved at the waitress to tell her we were ready for the check.

She dropped it on our table, thanking us for coming, and I grabbed it before Stef could. "All right. But I want pictures, or it didn't happen."

"What didn't happen?"

"Whatever—or whoever—it is that's so scandalous you can't tell me about it."

We gathered our coats and purses and stood to leave. "You're the only one with a scandalous love life, Ailee.

Wait until your ex finds out you're seeing someone half his age."

I jabbed my arm into my coat sleeve at the mention of "He Who Shall Not Be Named" and made a face. "Just seeing the look on his face would almost make it worth it."

"Please make sure I'm there when he finds out."

"I'll do my best."

"You're a true friend."

On the sidewalk outside the restaurant, we hugged before Stef headed to her apartment to work for the rest of the afternoon and I made my way to the bus stop. Parking was always such a nightmare, I avoided driving into the city whenever possible. Why fight all the traffic when the bus had a direct route from my little town to the section of Seattle where Stef lived? It even had its own lane all the way into the city.

Halfway there, I passed by Whole Foods and decided to make a quick stop. My fridge was pretty empty and avoiding the grocery store on a weekend was something I strove for. Though I would probably have to make a run for the heavier items I didn't want to lug onto the bus.

I made a face at the thought of two grocery trips in the same amount of days, eliciting a strange look or two from other customers. Smiling at them, I grabbed a basket and headed to the produce section. I was just rounding the floor display of avocados when I saw him.

Tyler was standing not twenty feet away from me, a basket hanging from one arm as he searched for the perfect orange.

Unsure of what to do or how to react, I stood frozen, watching him load up on citrus. When he stepped around to select from a different side, I noticed for the first time what he was wearing.

Tyler was dressed all in black, from his head to his toes. His T-shirt was too big, baggy sweats with pockets on the legs hung low on his lean hips, and a black beanie covered his head. The only color was the white soles of his Converse and the words "Nope. Not Today." on the front of his shirt. The look was strange on him, but not anything half the guys in the city weren't wearing, albeit the younger crowd. Like, quite a bit younger.

I didn't know why I hadn't noticed how strangely he was dressed earlier. Or, maybe this was how he always dressed when he wanted to play it down. As I stared, trying to decide if I should put him on the spot and say hello or not, a tall, thin female with a head of cottony blonde hair joined him. She laughed when she saw the pile of oranges in his basket and grabbed his arm to drag him away.

Willow.

It had to be.

He pulled away from her to grab one more and added it to the basket. His eyes lifted and met mine across the groups of produce.

I smiled and gave him a little wave, trying to act natural.

His brown eyes grew wide and his mouth dropped open in an almost childlike manner when he saw me. He didn't wave back. Instead, he reached behind him without taking his eyes from me and tapped Willow on the arm. When she turned toward him, he leaned over and whispered something in her ear. Red flooded his cheeks as she turned to see who he was talking about.

Feeling as embarrassed as he looked, I tried to think of a way to retreat gracefully. With another little wave, I dropped my gaze and turned on my heel to make my escape.

"Ailee?"

I stopped at the sound of her voice. It was as breezy as her hair. When I turned back around, they were both coming toward me.

She said something to him as they neared, something I couldn't hear, right before she stuck out her long, narrow hand. "Hi! You're Ailee. The photographer, right? Tyler has told me so much about you."

I took her hand and returned her smile. I couldn't help it. Much as I wanted to hate her, the woman exuded warmth and friendliness, almost like we were old friends. "Yes. And you're Willow?"

She nodded and gave my hand a squeeze before she dropped it. "I'm Tyler's sister."

I looked up at Tyler. "Hey."

He pulled his beanie off. "Hi, Ailee," he said. He still looked nervous, but not in a "I just blew you off for a week" kind of way. It was more of a kid who has a crush on his teacher kind of nervousness. "How ya doin?"

His voice sounded weird, a little higher than normal and with a bit of an urban feel to it. Was he high or something? "Um, I'm good. Thanks. Stef and I actually saw you about an hour or two ago, crossing the intersection. We said hi, but maybe you didn't hear us?" As soon as the words were out of my mouth, I could've kicked myself. He was acting strange enough, and it was obviously, because he was trying to blow me off. Putting him on the spot about it didn't do anything except make this whole thing more awkward.

He touched the tip of his nose. Not cocky-like. A nervous tick. "Oh, uh. Yeah. Sorry about that. I didn't see you."

My eyes went to his hair, sticking from his head in all directions. It hadn't struck me earlier, maybe because it was so windy, but now I realized it was intentionally styled that way. Willow took over the conversation then, pulling my eyes away from his new do. "So, what are you doing in the city? Tyler told me you live out toward Snoqualmie?"

"I do," I told her. "I just came into the city to have lunch with a friend, and thought I'd pick up a few things before I headed back to the studio."

"I've seen your photos of Ty! And they're amazing. I wish I were that creative. How did you get into the business?"

She spoke so fast her words kinda all ran together, and it took me a moment to catch up. "Um, well…" I kept one eye on Tyler as we got into a discussion of my budding hobby when I was married, and how I'd turned it into a successful business after my divorce.

"That's amazing. No wonder Tyler thinks the world of you. Brains and beauty."

It occurred to me that she kept talking about Tyler as if he wasn't standing right next to her. As for him, he kept giving me little, shy smiles, looking away and touching his nose, his other hand with the beanie half shoved into the pocket of his hoodie. He didn't say much at all during the entire conversation.

I didn't get it. It was Tyler, and yet it was…not. There were little things that were throwing me off. Things other people might not notice, but I did.

This whole situation was just entirely too weird. "Well, um. I really need to go, or I'll miss my bus and have to wait for the next one."

"It was great to meet you," Willow said. "Hopefully, next time we'll get to hang out a little more."

"Sure, that would be great." I turned to the stranger at her side. "See ya, Tyler."

"Bye, Ailee."

Willow elbowed him. The movement was small, but I noticed it.

"I'll call you soon," he told me. "I'm sorry I've been kind of MIA. I'll explain when I see you again."

"It's okay. I've been busy, too. Nice to meet you, Willow." I gave them both a small smile and headed toward the exit. Abandoning my basket with its lone avocado at the door, I rushed to the bus stop, making it just as a bus pulled up. I didn't know if it was my bus or not. I didn't care. I just had to get out of there.

Once the door closed and we were speeding east down 19, I pulled out my phone and texted Stef to fill her in.

Also, I'd forgotten to tell her Willow's name.

I was rewarded with laughing emojis and GIFS the rest of the way home, though I made sure to admonish her, telling her she was actually really nice.

For reasons I wasn't sure of myself, I didn't tell her about how strange Tyler had been acting.

CHAPTER 9

Tyler

I woke up in jerks, like something had a hold of my ankle and was trying to yank me back down into the abyss. Struggling to free myself, I would rip it free and manage to swim up a few feet, only to be jerked down again.

In the end, I won the battle, waking up the rest of the way all at once in a wicked rush, my heart pounding and my legs and arms shaking with fatigue like I'd just escaped death itself. I blinked hard, and my vision gradually cleared.

I was on a plush red couch wearing a white blanket that covered everything but my feet. Sweat stuck my shirt to my spine and trickled down my temples into my hair, and when I shoved off the blanket and swung my legs around to sit up, I could see why. I was wearing sweatpants along with a T-shirt instead of sleeping in my boxer briefs like I normally did. Also, there was a black and white cat curled up on my stomach. Or, at least, it had been. He toppled to my lap when I sat up, then jumped down to the floor. Giving me a glare for tossing him off his bed in such a reckless manner, he sauntered off to the kitchen to find his food dish.

My heart stuttered in my chest, then picked up again, beating out a furious rhythm. I didn't remember putting these clothes on. I didn't remember even owning these clothes.

Leaning forward, I stuck my head between my knees and focused on the here and now, breathing deep and even until I could form a coherent thought again. I was in a large apartment with an open concept floor plan. Colorful tapestries covered the walls, and other than the red couch, the rest of the furniture was a mishmash of styles and colors, including the four completely different kitchen chairs surrounding the small round table separating the kitchen and the living room, where I had apparently been napping.

If the cat hadn't been enough to tip me off, the bohemian décor would've told me where I was. I was in Willow's apartment. I was safe. And I didn't stink like alcohol.

Relief washed over me. It was hard to admit even to myself, but I'd really been thinking I was some kind of closet alcoholic. So secret, I didn't even know it myself until I woke up from the latest binge.

The cat came back over to me and rubbed against my legs, loud purrs rumbling from his little body. Obviously, I'd been forgiven for waking him so abruptly. "Good morning to you, too, Sir Elton," I told him as I rubbed his cheeks. I didn't blame him for being grouchy. I was grouchy too when I had to wake up before I was ready.

My sister was a huge fan of Sir Elton John. Always had been, as far back as I could remember. When we were kids, she'd had a turtle named Rocket Man, and a doll she'd called Levon. Levon was a girl, but that didn't seem to faze Willow.

I think the real Elton would have approved, in any case.

Her cat, which she'd adopted from a shelter, had been chosen out of all the others because he was "a distinguished gentleman, who could pull off a tuxedo but was still a playful fellow who enjoyed wearing costumes" just like her favorite entertainer. Of course, no other name would do for him.

Sir Elton flicked his white-tipped tail, gave me one last degrading look, and disappeared around the side of the cabinets. A second later, I heard his tags clinking on his food dish as he ate.

"Oh! You're up!"

Willow came out of her room, the only bedroom in the place. She was the picture of conservative office wear in tan slacks, a white blouse, and low, black heels. Her face was fresh looking, and her hair was tamed into loose waves that fell just past her shoulders. But her expression was tense as she walked slowly into the room. "Tyler?"

I cocked an eyebrow at her. "Willow?"

She just stared at me, like she expected me to jump up and start trashing the place or something.

My head hurt, and my chest was beginning to ache. I wasn't in the mood for her games. "What the fuck? Why are you being so weird?"

Her thin shoulders relaxed, and she smiled. "Sorry." She checked the watch on her wrist. "You want some coffee?"

"What time is it?"

"It's 7:25," she called over her shoulder as she went to the kitchen.

"Why am I here?" I managed to keep my tone pretty neutral, but I couldn't stop my voice from shaking. "I don't remember coming over." I tried to laugh it off. "Maybe I need more sleep."

She didn't answer me. I heard the coffee machine brewing, and then the door to the fridge open and close. A few seconds later, she came back in with two mugs. She handed one to me, then sat down in the chair nearest me.

"I don't remember coming here," I repeated, and there was no humor in my voice this time. I wrapped both hands around the cup and let the warmth seep into me, trying to fight the chill that had settled into my bones. I couldn't bring myself to look at her. "Willow, what am I doing here?"

Her voice was just as quiet as mine. "You've been sleeping here, Ty."

"Why aren't I sleeping at my own place?" My place. Shit. I set the mug down on the end table beside me. "I have to go check on Snickers."

Willow grabbed my arm with surprising strength before I could stand up. "He's fine. I hired that dog sitter you like. The one you use when you go out of town. And don't worry," she continued when I gave her a surprised look. "I'll pay for him."

I sat back down. Hard. This time, I couldn't take my eyes off my sister's face. I tried to ask what I wanted to ask, but nothing came out. I stopped, swallowed, closed my eyes, opened them, and tried again. "How long have I been here?"

She gave me that big sister look. The one she always gives me when she wants to fix the bad stuff and can't.

"Willow." My tone was harsh, but I needed to know.

"Five days," she told me quietly.

Five. Days.

No, that couldn't be right.

I searched her face, looking for signs she was joking.

Please, tell me you're joking.

But something within me, some inner time clock, told me she wasn't.

Holy FUCK.

Almost an entire week of my life.

Spots started dancing in front of my eyes, and the edges of my vision blurred. Pain lanced through my chest. I couldn't breathe. A voice yelled at me through a fog. A male voice.

Not my own.

"Tyler! Tyler, stay with me. Focus on me." My sister's face appeared in my line of vision. She smiled. "Stay here. We need to talk."

I gripped her thin arms, pulling her closer, listening to her voice. The abyss was reaching for me again, but I didn't want to go. I needed to stay here. I needed to hear what she had to say.

"Just breathe. In and out."

I did as she told me, clearing my mind of everything but her voice as I fought against the vice around my chest. After a minute or so, my heart stopped racing, and the darkness began to recede. It worked. I was surprised to find my cheeks wet with tears. "Willow. Help me. You have to help me. I don't know what the fuck is going on. I don't know what the fuck..." I drifted to a halt as a sob tore from my chest.

"Shhhh." She grabbed my face between her palms. "You're okay. You're fine. Just breathe. You need to calm down, and then we can talk."

But suddenly, I didn't want to hear what she was going to tell me. Because I knew that whatever it was, it was going to change things forever. And I wasn't ready for that. I pulled out of her grip and stood, shaking my head. Spotting my cell phone and my wallet on the kitchen counter, I sidestepped Willow and headed toward it, my steps determined, if not very steady.

"Tyler! Where are you going?"

"Home." I grabbed up my wallet, checked that my bus card was in there, shoved my phone in my front pocket, and then I was out the door before she could stop me. I heard her calling me, but as soon as I hit the pavement, I took off running.

It wasn't until I was on the bus and it was rumbling through the city that I realized I didn't have any shoes on.

As soon as I got home, I tore off the ruined socks on my feet and chucked them into the kitchen trashcan. The clothes I'd slept in soon followed. No one was there, so I walked naked back to my bedroom and got into the shower. I scrubbed my skin until it was red and raw, from my scalp to my toes. Not sure what I was trying to accomplish there, but I had this overwhelming need to rid myself of whoever the fuck I'd been the past week. Only when I was clean and in my own clothes again did I start to feel normal.

I was sitting at the kitchen table with a notepad, making notes of all the weird shit that had been happening to me lately, when the front door opened and Snickers came trotting in. He did a little dance when he saw me, and bounded in my direction, squirming up into my lap.

"Hey, buddy. Hey. I know. I missed you, too." Squinting through the dog kisses, I saw Todd, my dog sitter, closing the door and setting Snickers's leash on the counter. "Hey," I greeted him. "Thanks so much for coming on short notice." I assumed it was short notice, because I sure as hell hadn't made any plans to black out for five days.

Todd laughed as I try to avoid getting a dog tongue across my nose. "No problem! Snickers is my favorite pup. He was a great boy, as usual."

I gave my best friend one last squeeze and set him down on the floor, watching as he trotted over to his water dish. "What do I owe you, man?"

But Todd shook his head. "Not a thing. Your sister already paid me. How was your trip?"

"It was great." I avoided his eyes as I stood to show him out.

He took the hint and gave Snickers a scratch and a wave, then turned to leave. "Anytime you need me, just call. I've always got time for you guys."

"Thanks again." I shut the door behind him with a sigh of relief, and was again left alone with my thoughts. So far, I'd managed to keep the panicky feelings at bay, but I didn't know how long that was going to last. I also didn't know what the hell was happening to me or when it would happen again.

What I did know was that I couldn't keep ignoring it.

I made a cup of coffee, since I'd never drank the one Willow had made me, then went into the living room where my laptop was charging beside the couch. With Snickers snuggled up beside me, I got online and found my doctor's website. It must be a busy time of year, because they couldn't fit me in for another ten days.

I could last ten days. It was all good. I could do this. Maybe I should get some kind of medic alert bracelet - "If found, please call this number."

"Ah, God." It wasn't even funny, that was the sad part.

I stared at the table of available appointment times, and then I closed the laptop without making one. I knew it was stupid to put it off. But I was scared. And I was a fucking coward. I just...didn't want to know. And somewhere deep down, I still hoped this would all somehow just go away and go back to normal.

Setting my laptop on the coffee table, I rubbed my forehead with my fingertips, massaging the constant ache I'd had there since I'd woken up at Willow's. I needed to call Ailee. What the fuck must she be thinking? First, I run out on her at her studio. Then I finally get her to agree to give me another chance, and promptly fall off the face of the earth. I had no idea if I'd already called her or seen her in the past five days.

That would be good to know.

There was no help for it. I needed to call my sister.

Ripping the Band-Aid off, I hit her name on my contact list.

"Hello? Tyler? Are you okay?"

"I'm fine. Did I have any contact with Ailee while—" What? I was out of it? "While I was at your place? Was I there the entire time?"

"Tyler, we need to talk about things—"

"Just answer the fucking question, Willow." I took a breath and softened my tone. "Please. Just...just answer the question."

After a brief pause, she said, "You were with me the entire time. You ran into her once while we were doing some shopping."

"That's it?" What the fuck had I said?

"That's it."

"You're sure?"

"I'm positive. You were with me the whole time, Ty. It's okay."

"Yeah, you keep fucking saying that." I heard her muffled voice talking to someone. She must've gone into work. "Hey, you're busy, and I have to go. Thanks."

"Tyler, wait—"

I hung up the phone. But as soon as I did, I sent her a quick text. She didn't deserve the way I was treating her. But I just couldn't talk about it. Not right now. Right now, I just wanted to pretend everything was normal. I wanted to call Ailee. I wanted to take her out. I wanted to buy her shit she didn't need, steal kisses, and lose my soul in her gorgeous blue eyes.

That was all I could handle right now.

CHAPTER 10

Ailee

The next day, I was getting ready to head down to the studio when my phone rang. I was in my closet looking for my favorite yoga pants to wear. It was Friday, and I was only going there to go over some accounting stuff and wasn't expecting to see anyone. I found them on the shelf hiding behind some jeans and made it to my phone right before voicemail picked up. It was lying face down on the bed, and I picked it up, hitting the accept call button without looking as I sat down and started pulling on my pants over my pink underwear. "Hello?"

"Hey, Ailee."

I froze with one leg in and one leg out as the husky, deep tones of Tyler's voice brought goose bumps to my skin.

"Hey." I'd just seen him the day before, and the meeting had been pretty anti-arousing. So why was I reacting this way now? I abandoned the whole getting dressed thing for the moment and cleared my throat. "What's up?" Good. That sounded casual enough.

"I was wondering if you're free tonight. I'd like to take you out on that date I promised you." He waited for a response. "Ailee?"

I couldn't respond right away. This guy, this confident, sexy guy I could feel over the phone, was the Tyler I knew. But my brain kept bouncing back and forth between the man I was talking to and the guy I saw at the store yesterday.

"Ailee? Are you there?"

"Um, yeah. Yes. Sorry. Bad connection." I rolled my eyes at the lame excuse. Even I wouldn't believe myself.

"I was asking if you'd like to go to dinner tonight."

My loins tightened at the thought of seeing him, even after all of the weirdness of the day before. I had a flash of this Tyler staring at me hungrily through the glass door of my apartment building. I didn't know where that guy was yesterday, but I wanted to see him again. "Um, yeah. That sounds great."

"I can pick you up at your place around six. Unless you'd be more comfortable meeting me somewhere?"

"Uh, no, I'll meet you outside at six. That sounds good."

The smile he was wearing came across loud and clear in his voice. "Great. Perfect. I can't wait to see you again." A pause. "It's been way too long. And again, I apologize for disappearing the way I did. Um, I'll explain more tonight."

"Tyler, that's not necessary. Really." I didn't know why I was giving him an out. Maybe I didn't want to be too involved in his life, and like Stef kept telling me, I was holding myself back. Or maybe I just didn't want to know something that would threaten whatever this was blooming between us.

Because despite my hesitancy, I kinda fucking liked it.

"I'll see you tonight, Ailee."

His words held a promise I intended to hold him to. I needed to stop flipping back and forth on this. I liked Tyler. I was attracted to him, and then some. I wanted to get to know him better. A LOT better. I didn't know what had happened yesterday. Maybe he'd acted weird because his sister was there and he hadn't told her about me yet. Maybe there'd been some kind of family discussion going on and I'd interrupted it. I didn't know. But I'd give him a chance to explain.

Decision made, a thrill zipped through me. "See you tonight." After we hung up, I sat there for a few minutes, staring at the blank screen of my phone. Emotions I hadn't felt in a long time crashed around inside of me—excitement, dread, arousal, fear—and in a brief moment of panic, I almost called him back and cancelled. But in the end, I finished getting dressed and went down to my studio.

I spent the remainder of the day firmly pushing Tyler from my mind and concentrating on work stuff. Not an easy task while dealing with numbers. I wasn't a math person, and doing the necessary bookkeeping for my business tended to make my eyes glaze over even on a good day. I really needed to hire an assistant to do this for me. I could afford it. Only the task of going through the process of finding someone I liked and trusted held me back.

Four hundred and seventy-three years later, my books were balanced, and it was time to go home and get ready for my date. A cold drizzle was falling, and autumn was definitely in the air. Typical for September. I smiled to myself. I loved this time of year in the Pacific Northwest, despite the constant rain. It was cold enough to feel like autumn, and if I wanted snow for Christmas, all I had to do was drive about fifteen minutes down the road into the Cascade Mountains.

In the hall, I said hi to my neighbors, a young couple with a new baby, and let myself into my apartment. Setting my bag down on the table, I carefully kept my mind blank as I got a cup and a tea bag out of the cupboard. I made my tea, but it did nothing to warm the chill in my bones, so I decided to jump in the shower to warm up.

The warm water jolted my sensitive skin the moment I stepped under the spray, making it quite obvious to me that Tyler wasn't as far from my thoughts as I liked to believe. I moaned aloud. I hadn't felt this alive in years, and in spite of my recent decision about Tyler, I both reveled in it and resented it.

Ever since my divorce, I'd been shut down sexually. And that had been fine by me. I didn't have time to sit around pining for a man to make me feel good. Instead, I was too busy turning the hobby my ex-husband had scoffed at into a business successful enough to support me fully. I still didn't have time. I had a business to run and a life to live. A life I'd chosen. A life I loved.

I frowned as I wet my hair. Actually, that was wrong. It had happened years before we legally separated. My husband hadn't been easy to live with, though I think he'd cared about me as much as he could, and I now realized I'd stayed with him a lot longer than I should have. It was such a cliché, but I'd done it for the kids. However, I often wondered if I'd done them more harm than good by letting them grow up watching two people in such a stagnant relationship. I could only pray they were smart enough to know that our marriage hadn't been anything resembling a healthy relationship, and it's not something they should strive for in their own relationships. If I'd been any kind of a mother at all, I would've left him right after our first was born and taken him out of that toxic environment. But instead, I'd smiled through the hurt—

both emotional and, at times, physical—and pretended everything was fine.

I was really good at that.

As I ran the shower puff over the front of my body, I ignored the way my nipples puckered and ached at the slightest touch. And I absolutely, positively, did not let my soapy fingers linger between my legs, inserting them into the sensitive folds until my heart was pounding and my breath was coming in pants as the ache in my lower belly grew in waves.

And I seriously did not imagine it was Tyler touching me.

Grinding my teeth together, I pushed the fantasy from my mind and forced my hand away as I finished my shower. But no matter how much I fought it, the memory of his heated gaze lingered, heating my blood.

Was I doing the right thing, agreeing to see him? My doubts were still there, in large white font, on those red flags that were still waving away.

And no matter what he might say, he had doubts, too. Why else would he have stopped kissing me the night of the shoot? He'd looked at me like he'd had no idea who I was, or what he was doing there.

Well, buddy, that made two of us.

With all of this shit bouncing around in my head and feeling so horny I was afraid I'd embarrass myself, I came really close to calling Tyler and cancelling our date tonight. But in the end, I dried my hair in messy waves and got dressed. Nothing too fancy, just jeans, my favorite boots, and a soft, pale mauve, long-sleeved sweater. Some minimal makeup, my jacket with the big hood, and I was ready for the rain.

And whatever else might happen.

Fingers crossed.

I tried to think about what Stef would do. She was always telling me I needed to get out more, have some fun. And maybe she was right. My life was all work and no play. What would it hurt to have a little casual fun with a guy who made me feel good? Someone who made me feel young, like a woman again. I should stop overthinking everything and just go with it for however long it lasted, which probably wouldn't be very long at all, given my history with men.

But as soon as I pushed open the door to my building and saw Tyler standing in the rain, waiting for me—for *me*—I knew I was only trying to fool myself. There was nothing casual at all about my feelings for this man.

He was dressed all in black again, but not in sweats. Oh no. This time, he wore jeans that hugged his powerful legs, black boots with thick soles, and a stylish black raincoat that came almost to mid-thigh. His hair was damp. His eyes burned through me. And I felt the surge of desire that rushed through him at my appearance on the stoop reverberate in me. This man was too much, a fantasy from my deepest, darkest desire come to life.

When I could only stand there and stare, one side of his mouth lifted in a cocky smile and his eyes darkened as they raked over me from head to toe.

Good God.

Taking a deep breath to steady myself, I joined him on the sidewalk. I had little choice, really. I was drawn to him like a magnet. "Hey." My voice was a little shaky, but I lifted my chin in defiance of my failing courage.

"Are you ready?"

Chills ran through me at those three simple words. Was I? "Yeah, I'm ready." As ready as I'd ever be.

He made no move to leave as his eyes travelled over my face and hair, then dropped down to the front of my conservative sweater beneath my open jacket. That little, secretive smile appeared again, and it hit me that my unwitting attempt to hide a part of myself from him—even if it was just my cleavage—had backfired completely. When his gaze gradually drifted back to mine, the carnal heat burning within brought a rush of blood to my cheeks.

Despite the promises darkening his eyes, he shoved his hands into his front pockets, and I noticed he did that a lot around me. A nervous reaction? Or to keep from touching me? My ego preferred to think it was the latter.

"Look," he told me, his voice a bit gruff. "I know this has all been a bit...intense. This thing between us. So, I thought it would be good to go somewhere fun and just, I don't know, hang out."

"Oh, okay," I said.

But I don't think I successfully hid my surprise, because he smiled again and reached out with one hand to tuck my hair back behind my ear. "We have lots of time, Ailee."

He was lying. I felt it all the way to my bones.

But, why would that be a lie? We did have time. At least some. I wasn't quite that old. I mean, I wasn't one foot in the grave or anything, but I wasn't a young girl, either. I smiled back at him to hide my growing disappointment. Which was weird, considering I'd been ready to call off this whole thing less than an hour ago. "What did you have in mind?"

Instead of answering me, he held out his hand. "Come on."

I slid my cold fingers through his. He held on tight, covering our joined fingers with his other hand to warm them before we started walking. My mind went resolutely blank as we walked down the street, and I kept my focus on putting one foot in front of the other without tripping over the cracks in the sidewalk. It took me a minute to realize we were headed to the bus stop. "We're taking a bus?"

He glanced down at me, his expression unsure. "I hope that's okay."

He looked so frazzled by my question, I hurried to reassure him. "Yeah! Yeah, that's fine. I take the bus all the time. I'm just surprised, is all."

"Yeah, um. I don't drive. Never got my driver's license. And living here, I don't need to. Public transportation gets me anywhere I want to go. The only time it sucks is when it's really raining. But I'm pretty used to it. This is Seattle, after all."

We stepped under the shelter. There was only one other person there, an older man who was half-asleep on the bench. "So, Willow seems nice," I said.

Tyler checked the time on his phone and then shoved it back into the pocket of his rain jacket. He seemed distracted when he answered me. "You met Willow?"

Those red flags, previously weighted down by the urgency of my sexual needs, gave a flap. "Uh, yeah. I saw you guys in the city, at Whole Foods. Remember?"

He looked confused for a moment, but then his expression cleared, and a smile broke out. "Oh yeah! That's right. I almost forgot." But his eyes were guarded.

"Tyler? What's going on?"

"What do you mean?"

I pulled my fingers from his and took a step back as I shoved my hands into the pockets of my raincoat. "You know exactly what I mean. Something's weird with you, and if we're going to be 'dating,'"—I made air quotes with my fingers—"then I think I deserve to know what's going on. I'm too old for head games, and I don't have the time or the energy to play guessing games or sneak around."

"What makes you think I'd ask you to sneak around? Who would we be hiding from?"

"I don't know. But something is going on, and I want to know what it is, or I'm not leaving this bus stop."

Right on cue, the bus pulled up with a squeak of its brakes. The doors hissed loudly as they opened and a small group of people piled out, pulling up their hoods to protect them from the rain.

Tyler glanced at the bus and then back at me, his gaze a little frantic. "I swear to you I'll explain everything. But first, I just..." He closed his eyes, exhaling loudly. When he opened them, he was once again calm and collected. "I just want to have a fun night first. A fun night with you. Can we do that?"

My heart dropped as I stared at him with suspicion I didn't even try to hide.

He walked to the bus and waited for me to get in first. I glanced at the bus driver, then back to Tyler.

Why did I suddenly feel like this was a goodbye date?

CHAPTER 11

Tyler

The bus took us to the Snoqualmie Casino. As we pulled up to the front doors, Ailee turned to me with a quizzical look.

"We're gambling?"

That wasn't why I'd brought her here, but I'd come prepared with funds. Just in case. "Sure, if you want."

She turned away to peer out the window. "Believe it or not, I've never been here."

"Really? Never? You live, like, ten minutes away." Hard to believe, but secretly I was thrilled that it would be her first time. No matter what happened between us, if she ever came here again, she would remember being here with me.

I planned to make this night unforgettable.

"I don't exactly have money to throw away on slots."

"Well, there's other stuff to do here, too. There are a few different restaurants and a show a little later I've got tickets for."

"What kind of a show?"

I stood and held out my hand. "You'll see."

She eyeballed me for a few seconds, but I stayed steady, and in the end she took my hand and allowed me to lead her from the bus.

Inside, I was hit from all sides by the delightful gaudiness of the place, the bright red and gold decor a perfect match with the clink of coins being dropped into a hundred slot machines, audible even over the music streaming through the sound system and the low roar of laughter and shouts from the other patrons. Flashing lights halfway blinded me, and cigarette smoke burned my lungs. All in all, a perfect distraction from my problems.

I started coughing. "I completely forgot people can smoke here," I croaked out. Ailee wasn't faring much better. "We can go somewhere else," I told her when I could manage it. "If you'd like."

She shook her head. "No, it's okay. You said you bought tickets for the show. I'll survive one night." She waved her hand in front of her face as the lady in front of the nickel slots beside us blew a cancerous cloud in our direction as she looked around, presumably for the waiter to bring her another drink. "However, now I remember why I don't hang out here."

I grabbed her hand again and tugged her away, and we hightailed it out of there and headed to a side of the casino where the air was distinctly clearer. "So, what do you want to do first?" I asked her when we could breathe again.

Her free hand went to her stomach. "Um...food would be good."

I grinned down at her and squeezed her hand. "A woman after my own heart."

We picked the place with an all-you-can-eat buffet and I let her go in front of me, watching with amusement as she piled her plate high. It was fucking refreshing. I wondered if she'd be as free with her choices if it wasn't a buffet. I hoped so. People needed to eat, and I was one hundred percent about keeping those luscious curves on her well filled out.

We ate in silence, both of us digging into our dinner with gusto. I didn't know about her, but I was fucking starving. It was a good five minutes later when I noticed she'd laid down her fork and was eying me with a thoughtful look on her face. "What?" I asked around a mouthful of pasta.

"I was just wondering if maybe we should lay down some rules."

I almost choked on my mac and cheese. "Rules?" I set down my fork and gave her my full attention. This should be interesting. "What kind of rules?"

"Dating rules."

"Dating rules," I repeated. I didn't laugh, although it took some effort.

A blush crept up her neck to her cheeks, but her chin rose in defiance of my obvious enjoyment. "Yes, Tyler. Rules. I want to know—"

"What my intentions are toward you?" I kept my face suitably stoic.

She tilted her head to give me a look of disdain, her dark hair falling like strands of silk over her shoulder. "I have questions I want to ask you, but first I want to know how personal I should get," she clarified. "Because I've had my heart torn apart before, and I'd rather avoid it happening again, if at all possible. So, I know you said let's date and just see what happens, but if you're planning to keep this...whatever it is between us on the casual side, I really need to know that up front. I just want to know what to expect, and then I can handle whatever gets thrown at me."

Ah. She was talking about her ex-husband. And the flash of pain in her eyes made me want to hunt the asshole down and smash his head through one of those slot machines.

There were a lot of things I could've said in this instance. Flowery things. Things that would take off the pressure. Things that would leave her guessing.

But I couldn't do any of that. I couldn't bullshit her. Not with her sitting over there looking so damn tough and yet so damn fragile.

I set down my fork, took a sip of soda, and wiped my mouth with the napkin. Then, I scooted out of the booth nice and easy like and went over to her side. I gestured for her to move over with a lift of my chin, and then I slid in beside her.

I wanted to pull her to me, wrap her up in my arms and hold her until those echoes of her past life were gone from her eyes. I wanted to lay her back in this booth and kiss her senseless. I wanted her to forget any other man that had come before me.

But I didn't do any of that, because something told me what she needed right now was raw honesty, not a distraction. So, that's what I gave her.

Grasping her chin firmly, I turned her face fully toward me and forced her to meet my eyes. And then I said very clearly, "I don't know what's going to happen with us, Ailee. And if I remember correctly, it wasn't me, but you, who kept insisting you didn't want anything serious to happen between us. Playing it cool and asking you if we could just date was the only way I could think of to get you to agree to spend more time with me. But keeping it casual was never my plan, and if I'm gonna be completely honest here, it's not possible for me at this point in any case. Because, you see," I paused, searching her face for any indication that this was too much. But there was nothing in her wide blue eyes telling me to stop. "I'm already half in love with you." Even I could hear the nervous tremor in my voice, and I shook my head against the sudden pain in my temple. "I don't think it's your heart in danger of breaking." I put everything out there. Let it all show. "It's mine."

She stared at me, probably wondering if I wasn't just a little bit insane. And she was probably right. My feelings for her were intense, but there wasn't much I could do about it.

With a little sound of amusement that was aimed completely at myself, I kissed the tip of her nose, then released her face and indicated the uneaten food on her plate. "Eat. I'm paying good money for this food." Back on my own side of the booth, I picked up my fork and started eating like I hadn't just made a profound announcement she totally wasn't expecting.

After a moment, she slowly picked up her own utensil and followed suit. We shared a few looks—mine amused and hers a bit shell-shocked, but I had effectively shut down any other efforts at conversation with my little speech.

I was the one who broke the silence. "So, go ahead, Ailee. Ask me whatever you want."

She speared me with a startled look, then looked around like someone else might remember what it was she'd wanted to ask before focusing back on me. "What do you do when you're not modeling?"

Stuffed, I pushed my plate aside, and settled into the corner of the seat. "You want to know if I'd be able to provide for you."

"No," she corrected. "I don't need you, or anyone, to provide for me. I want to know if you can provide for yourself."

Feisty. I liked feisty. "So, you're asking me if I'm looking for a sugar momma."

"Exactly."

I laughed out loud. "Nope. That's not my motive here. Modeling is just a hobby for a little extra cash. As you know, unless I was selling a lot more shots for covers, I wouldn't survive the month."

"So, how do you survive?"

By the skin of my teeth these days. "Well, I told you I was in school. I get some extra money through my loans and grants."

"What else?"

Smart lady. Modeling and school loans together still wouldn't pay for even an itsy-bitsy apartment in Seattle. Maybe if I had a one room loft and ten roommates.

I pressed my lips together, squinting against the sharp pain in my head. "Um. I have some money in savings." Enough so I could not work for a good six months or so, actually. I pressed my fingers against my temples.

"You don't have a regular job?"

"I do some freelance work." I took a deep breath and pushed away the discomfort with sheer force of will. Gradually, the pain in my head eased up. I should've taken something before I left the house, but these headaches had been subsiding. I dropped my hand back into my lap and concentrated on Ailee. I didn't want to think about this shit right now. "Mostly admin type stuff. I'm actually a virtual assistant for a few authors in the industry. It's flexible, so I can work around my classes." I shrugged. "It all adds up." This was true. I'd been working for five authors at the same time not long ago. They knew me from modeling and when I saw them putting out the call for help, I answered, thinking it would be a great gig for me until I could work out whatever the fuck was going on with me. I did everything from posting on social media to helping them with the legal jargon of being in business for themselves.

Unfortunately, due to these fucking lapses in memory, I'd lost two of them within the past six weeks. Not because they didn't need me, but because they couldn't depend on me getting their stuff done when they needed it. And that was completely on me.

"Huh." She avoided my eyes, leaning over to take a sip of her drink.

Why did I get the feeling she didn't quite approve of my job choice? I scoffed at my own attitude. She was right. Being a VA wasn't my thing. But I was working on that. "It's just while I'm in school."

She nodded, regrouped. "How much longer do you have in school?"

I popped a French fry into my mouth. "Four years. One more year to finish up my degree and then three years of law school. Fall semester just started." Not that I'd managed to make it to class yet.

"That's very dedicated for a guy like you."

"What's that supposed to mean?" I wasn't offended. More amused than anything. And curious as to what she would say.

She held her hands up in a sign of truce. "No, no. I didn't mean it that way. I just meant..." She shrugged, at a loss for words. "I don't know. You just don't seem like the studying type. Not that there's anything wrong with that type! It just doesn't seem like...you."

I leaned forward, my curiosity piqued. "And what kind of guy do you think I am, Ailee?"

She shifted in her seat, and somehow, I knew. I knew if we were anywhere but in this restaurant full of people who reeked like cigarettes and booze, I could find out that she was wet for me. My cock thickened and my nostrils flared with the memory of the scent of her skin.

"I don't know. You come across more like a guy who likes to work with his hands." Her cheeks flushed the moment the words came out of her mouth. "A blue-collar type...or something."

I leaned forward and dropped my voice to a husky growl. "I am *very* good with my hands, Ailee."

Her lips parted and her chest rose on a quick inhale.

"But that's only one of my many talents." With a wink, I sat back in the booth and grabbed another fry. I needed to lighten the mood, or I'd never be able to get up out of this booth without the whole place knowing how hard up I was.

The waiter came over with our check, breaking the last threads of tension.

"Are you finished?" I gestured to her empty plate.

Ailee nodded, and I paid the check with cash and gave it back to the waiter, thanking him. "Come on, 'lee. Let's go blow some money and have some fun."

For the next two hours, we donated my hard-earned modeling pay to the casino. I taught her how to play Blackjack, which she lost, and I won, and then we sat beside each other at the slot machines. We drank too much and laughed too hard, trading stories from our teens and twenties. I told her how old I was after she coerced it out of me with a smile and a touch, and she was really surprised. I wasn't as young as she'd thought. I was flattered to find out she thought I was still in my twenties, when I was actually thirty-four. Still a bit of an age difference, but not as bad as she'd first thought. But as I'd told her before, quite a few times, I honestly didn't give a shit about it.

Trying a different slot machine, she pulled the lever down and we watched the fruit spin around and around. When it stopped, three 7s were lined up across the front of the machine. I jumped up when bells started ringing and lights flashed in our eyes.

"You won!" I yelled when she just sat there frowning at the machine.

"I did?"

People all around us were staring. "You did!" Laughing, I pulled her out of her seat and spun her around, making both of us dizzy.

After collecting her winnings, I held her hand as we headed into the ballroom for the show. It was a natural thing for me, and I noticed she allowed me to take it now with barely any notice.

"I've never won anything before," she admitted.

"And on the penny slots, too. That's not a common thing."

"I know exactly what I'm going to spend these two hundred dollars on," she announced.

"Oh, yeah? What's that?"

"A bookkeeper. I hate doing the books."

"I can't say that I blame you, although that will only give you one for about...what? Two weeks?"

She scrunched up her face with thought, and I think it was the most adorable thing I'd ever seen.

"Yeah, I'll have to figure that one out later."

I led her into the ballroom. Small tables were set up with black tablecloths and cushioned chairs, two per table, set close together and angled toward the stage. We sat down toward the back just as the lights dimmed, and I helped her hang her jacket on the back of her chair before doing my own.

I leaned in so close I could smell the fresh scent of her shampoo. "I hope you like this."

She didn't have time to answer. Soft lights hit the stage as three guys and a girl dressed in classy punk took position behind their instruments. A sultry melody started, highlighted by the haunting strings of a violin. Five beats in, and I was lost to the music. The singer stepped up to the mic, a rugged-looking guy around my age. Raw and full of angsty pain, his voice filled the room. Chills broke out all over my body, and I couldn't take my eyes from him.

My arm was resting on the table, and I felt Ailee take my hand and squeeze. I glanced at our joined fingers. She felt it, too.

Another glass of wine appeared in front of me, and I absentmindedly picked it up and took a sip. The sweet notes of blackberries and chocolate slid down my throat, warming my insides and loosening my muscles. I switched the hand holding hers and put my arm behind her shoulders. She leaned back against me as I sang quietly along with the song. Words of heartache, and want, and desire, and loss.

The song ended, and for a moment, no one made a sound. Then earsplitting applause filled the room. I didn't join them. I didn't want to move. I had one of my favorite artists in front of me and the woman I wanted more than anything in the world snuggled up against my side. My head was quiet, and though I was halfway hard, my soul was at peace. I wasn't about to do anything to fuck that up.

The pianist played a few notes, and the room quieted again. The next song was different. Just as haunting. A controlled kind of chaos, like good sex, and I felt my body responding to the melody and the feeling of Ailee against me.

Music always affected me this way, especially when the songs call to the deeper, darker part of myself.

I pulled Ailee in even closer. She turned her face toward me, so close our lips would touch if I moved just a fraction of an inch. Her breath was warm on my face, sweetened from the wine.

I couldn't take my eyes off her. In the light of the candle, she was both darkness and light, calling to the shades of my soul. My hand drifted up to cup her jaw, and she turned into it and kissed the center of my palm.

I felt the heat of her lips all the way to my cock.

And took her mouth with mine.

CHAPTER 12

Ailee

"*D*o you like it?"

I didn't know if Tyler was talking about the music or his kiss. Either way, the answer was the same. "Yes."

He smiled, and our eyes connected. He was barely touching me, and yet heat flared between us that rivaled the flame of the candle. Somehow, we'd gone from goofing off like a couple of kids to being on the verge of spontaneous combustion if I didn't get his clothes off. And soon.

"Dance with me."

It wasn't a request.

I allowed him to guide me out of my chair and out to the cleared space in front of the stage. One other couple was already there, swaying to the sultry beat of the music. Tyler took me into his arms, pulling me tight against his hard body, and wrapped one arm around my waist. I placed one hand on his shoulder, the other entwined with his against his chest.

He was a good dancer, and he sang softly to me as we moved around the floor in tempo to the beat. I was lost. Lost in the music. Lost in the words. Lost in his smell.

Lost in Tyler.

And for once, I let it happen. I didn't think about the other people there, and what they might be thinking of the two of us together. I doubted anyone was paying attention anyway, not with the show the band was putting on. They didn't jump around the stage, didn't try to work up the crowd. They didn't have to. They were completely mesmerizing because you could hear and feel their pain and passion within the music. And the singer not only had an incredible voice, but an almost inhuman charisma. From the moment they'd started playing, I'd felt as though I were intruding on something very private and very personal.

On the dance floor with Tyler, with his voice harmonizing with the lead singer's in my ear and the music pulsing through my blood, I felt part of it all. With each note, every painful moment of my life came bubbling to the surface, every passion I kept firmly sequestered, every fantasy I was always too afraid to make a reality. I was living it all. Here.

With Tyler.

We danced for two more songs. By the end of it, my pulse was pounding, and I was nearly moaning with need every time Tyler's muscular leg slid between mine as we stepped in time around the floor. He adjusted his hold on me slightly, and I did moan a little that time when my breasts pressed against his chest. I wanted our dance to go on forever, and at the same time, I couldn't wait for it to release me from its lustful hold.

"Let's get out of here." Tyler searched my eyes in between songs.

I didn't even stop to think about it. "Okay."

Grabbing my hand, we went by the table and both grabbed our wine glasses, finishing off what was left. I didn't know about him, but I needed the courage. Tyler threw some cash on the table, grabbed both our coats, and dragged me behind him as he pulled me from the ballroom and out of the casino.

A light rain had started up again, but neither one of us paused. He didn't take me to the place the bus would stop, but around the side of the building. Once out of sight, he threw my jacket around my shoulders and pressed me against the wall. I groaned as he took my mouth, our teeth and tongues clashing. When that wasn't enough, I raised up on my toes, slid my hands down to his narrow hips, and pulled him closer to my aching core.

Bending his knees, he rolled his hips into mine, and we both moaned when his hard length rubbed against me.

Of their own accord, my hands slid under his shirt to the warm skin beneath. Hard muscle met my palms, tightening everywhere I touched. I wanted to feel every inch of him, *taste* every inch of him, and with that thought in mind, I reached to undo his jeans.

"Ailee." He moaned my name. "Ah, God. Let me take you somewhere less public."

I completely agreed with that plan. But first, I slid my hand down the front of his jeans and...holy shit. I found him, and he slid into my palm perfectly. He was soft and thick and hard. So hard. Moisture dripped from the tip, and I licked my lips, wanting nothing more than to taste him.

Tyler's hands were on my breasts over my sweater, and his lips were on my neck. Kissing. Biting. Working me up. I didn't know if it was the alcohol, the music, or both, but I was bound and determined to have this man. Tonight. Right now. Consequences be damned. I'd bemoan my slutty actions to Stef's perky ears tomorrow over mimosas.

With my free hand, I pushed on his chest until he took a step back. Cold rain hit my face and neck, cooling my already damp skin.

Tyler blinked hard, confusion marring his features until I pushed the flaps of his jeans open more and pulled him completely free. He pulsed in my hand, thick and hot, and his eyes widened when he realized what I meant to do.

Though my heart was pounding with more than lust, I ignored the voice in my head asking me what the hell I was doing and took him into my mouth. He was salty sweet and burning hot, his hands tight in my hair even as he tried to tell me to stop before someone saw us.

I scraped my teeth lightly along his length, and his hips bucked forward, sending him deeper into my mouth. Closing my lips around him, I reveled in the power flowing through me. I never knew it would feel this way, this empowering, to do this act to a man. I'd never done it to my husband. I'd never had the desire, and he'd never asked. Sex with him had been lukewarm at best. Just the basics.

Sex with Tyler was volcanic.

And we hadn't even gotten to the good part, yet.

"Ailee, you need to stop. Please." He moaned as he thrust into my mouth one more time before he tightened his hold on my head and pulled me away. I tried to shake him off, but he was having none of it. "That feels so fucking good, Ailee." The words were staggered around hard breaths. "You have no fucking idea, but I'm not coming in your mouth outside a casino in the rain."

Embarrassment swept through me. It was a learned reaction from my past relationship, and I recognized that. There was no reason for the shame I was feeling. I was a full-grown woman, and there was nothing wrong with two consenting adults enjoying each other's bodies. And yet, I felt like a teenager being turned away by my crush I'd finally managed to coerce into a dark corner at a party because he had no better options, but then decided I just wasn't worth it.

His hands came to either side of my face and he lifted my head, forcing me to look at him. "No, 'lee. Don't do that. Don't do that, sweetheart."

I tried to look away. Unable to say anything around all the thoughts cluttered in my head and my blood still screaming through my veins, needing release.

But he wouldn't let me. "Look at me. Look at me."

I raised my eyes, fighting back tears.

"This thing that's happening right here, this thing between us. God, Ailee. It's like nothing I've ever fucking experienced before. You make me feel like I would fight anyone who would dare to look at you the wrong way, and at the same time, I want to fall to my knees every time you walk into the room. There is nothing, *nothing*, I want more than to back you up against this wall and push deep inside of you, but I won't cheapen what we have by sharing this with anyone who might walk around the corner."

I finally found my voice. "I'd be okay with that."

He laughed, a rich, deep sound of pure joy that brought a smile to my face and set my heart to pounding.

When he finally sobered, he searched my face again. "Let's go find somewhere a little quieter where we can be alone."

"We can go to my place. It's closer."

He smiled and his eyes softened. "Yeah. Let's go to your place."

The bus ride home took three hundred and twenty years. Tyler sat in the aisle seat, with his body turned toward me to block the view of his hand working its way up my thigh and his eyes hungrily devouring my body. But eventually, I was opening the door to my apartment and Tyler was following me inside.

I took off my coat and laid it over the kitchen chair, then turned to watch Tyler as he did the same, feeling suddenly shy. "Would you like something to drink?"

He touched my jaw with his fingertips. "That would be great. Do you have any coffee?"

"I have tea?"

"That'll work."

After all the hot and heavy outside the casino, my anxiety was back. Tyler seemed to sense it, backing off and pulling out a chair. He sat down at my kitchen table, looking for all the world like he belonged there as I made our tea.

"So. How long were you married?"

His cup rattled as I set it down on the table, and a little of it sloshed onto the table. "Shit." I grabbed a sponge from the sink and brought it over along with my cup, which I managed to set down without spilling tea.

He took the sponge from me and cleaned it up himself. "Sorry. It's none of my business."

"No, no. It's just...I wasn't expecting to talk about that."

"We don't have to." He stood and took the sponge over to the sink. "We can talk about something else if you're not comfortable. I was just curious."

"No. It's okay. I don't mind." At least he'd managed to shock me out of my pre-sex anxiety. Like a bucket of ice water dumped over my head. "I was married for fourteen years."

He stared at me over the rim of his cup. "That's a long time." Taking a sip, he set his tea back on the table and wrapped his hands around the cup. Elbows on the table, he leaned toward me. "I have another question."

"What's that?"

He cocked his head to the side. "Are you ready for me? For someone else to be in your life?"

I narrowed my eyes. "Define 'ready.'" Then I smiled to break the tension as I stared into his dark eyes, steady on my face as he patiently waited for my answer. Was I ready? "I honestly don't know." I took a breath. "I worked really hard to be where I am now. Independent. Happy. I'm not sure I'm ready to give that up."

"Who says you would have to give any of that up, Ailee?"

I thought hard about that answer. Wouldn't I, though? If I had someone in my life again, I would lose a part of myself.

"What about your kids? What would they think about having someone like me in your life?"

Wow. This guy was really serious. He wasn't just trying to get me into bed. And I wasn't sure whether to be happy about that or disappointed. "I'm not sure. We've never really talked about the possibility of that happening."

"Do they live here? In the area?"

"One does. My son. He's twenty-three, and just got his degree. He's working at Amazon, as one does when they live in Seattle and they have a technical degree." I smiled, my pride showing through. My kids were nothing like me. They were smart and happy and just beginning their lives. "My daughter lives in Oregon. She's twenty-five, and the complete opposite of her brother. She bought some land and is living in a yurt."

His forehead scrunched up in confusion. "What the hell is a 'yurt?'"

"Like a teepee, but made of wood, basically." I shrugged. I didn't understand my daughter's life needs. But that was okay. I didn't have to get everything she did. I just had to support her decisions and be happy that she was happy. "She likes it. I was concerned at first, with her living on such a large property all by herself, but she isn't that far from town and the neighbors she does have tend to watch out for each other."

"What does she do out there in the wilderness?"

"I'm not really sure. Reads a lot?" I laughed. "The last I knew, she was waiting to get internet access." I looked down at my tea. "I haven't talked to her in a while."

I felt his eyes on me, but he didn't pursue the subject and I was glad. My daughter and I had a bit of a complicated relationship. I loved her and she loved me, but we were too different to really be friends. And too alike to really dislike each other.

"And what about your marriage?"

I tried to keep my tone blasé. "What about it?"

"It was a large part of your life. Are you doing okay?" He shook his head slightly at his own question. "Not money-wise. I know you're fine. You have your own studio and your own apartment, and I see food on your counter." He indicated the loaf of bread next to the microwave. "So, I know you're not starving." His smile fell, and he got serious again. "But, in here." He touched the center of his chest. "Are you okay?"

Out of nowhere, tears filled my eyes. Tyler was the first person—first man, I should say—to ever ask me that. I sniffed a little. "It was hard, breaking up my family. Even with the kids grown."

"So, it was your decision to end it."

"Yes. My husband wasn't easy to live with, and I wasn't happy."

A change overcame him, and I could practically feel anger emanating from him. Even his voice was different when he asked, "Did he hurt you?"

I laid my hand over his on the table, touched that he was so concerned. "No, it wasn't like that. Not all the time. It was worse. He ignored me. Except when he was talking down to me like I was beneath him."

Tyler blinked a few times, something battling behind his eyes.

"Tyler?" I wasn't afraid, despite the struggle I could plainly see within him. But, for a brief second, I could've sworn someone else was looking at me through Tyler's eyes. I started to pull away, but he grabbed my hand and held on tight.

After a moment, the shadows cleared, and he came back to me. "I'm sorry you were treated that way, Ailee. You deserve so much more."

That was so strange. For a few seconds, I could swear it wasn't Tyler sitting here with me at all. It wasn't the guy I saw at the grocery store, either.

It had been someone else entirely.

"Tyler, what just happened?"

CHAPTER 13

uck.

Fuck!

My heart was pounding so hard it felt like it was about to break through my ribcage. I fought back the freak out that was trying to make its way to the surface.

It just happened again.

I'd blacked out completely. Just for a few seconds was my best guess, since I was still sitting here at Ailee's table with her.

But it had happened.

All I remembered was Ailee talking about what a shithead her ex had been. Something started buzzing around in my head. No, not buzzing. More like a growl. A man's growl. At first, I'd thought it was me, and I tried to stop, but then I'd realized I wasn't making any noise. It was all in my head. A shiver ran down my spine. Then my head got all foggy, and I was being shoved over by something—or someone—else. It sounded fucking crazy remembering, but this was the first time I was aware of one of my episodes coming on like that.

"Tyler, what was that?"

I focused on Ailee. I was gripping her hand like a lifeline. "Sorry," I mumbled as I relaxed my fingers. But I didn't let go. Not completely. I felt like she was the only thing anchoring me to this world.

"Tyler, you're scaring me a little."

"No, no. Don't be scared." I scooted my chair closer to her. I needed to feel her against me. "Don't be scared," I repeated as I wrapped my free hand around hers. "Kiss me, Ailee. Please."

Her blue eyes were full of questions as they travelled over my face, trying to find answers I couldn't give her right now.

"Kiss me," I whispered.

After a brief pause, she did, closing the distance between us and touching her lips to mine. Her lips were warm and sweet from the tea, the taste and textures of her mouth beginning to feel so familiar to me. She brushed her lips along mine once, twice, and again, before she pulled away to study me with blue eyes that had darkened to stormy gray.

It was so fucking hard to hold myself back. But I did. I stayed where I was and let her decide what she wanted to do. I didn't think about anything. Especially not about the fuck show that had just happened in my head. I concentrated on Ailee and only on Ailee.

My patience was rewarded when she leaned back in and kissed me again. A little harder this time. And my heart began to pound when I felt the tip of her tongue touch my lower lip. A shy taste. I groaned, tightening my hand in her hair, and pulled her in closer to me as I deepened the kiss.

I kissed her for what felt like hours, one hand in her soft hair and the other entwined with her fingers. Emptying my head until I couldn't think of anything but feeling her skin against mine. Of what she would taste like if I laid her back on this rickety old table and spread her legs wide. Of what her body would feel like in my hands. Of how tight she would squeeze me if I bent her over and slid inside her as deep as I could go.

My cock, already thick and hard, swelled even more with the fresh surge of blood. I stood up, bringing her with me, my lips never leaving hers, and pressed her palm against the bulge in my pants so she could feel what she did to me. She rubbed along my length, gripping me in her small hand.

I couldn't breathe.

Breaking off the kiss, I leaned my forehead against hers. She was breathing hard. As hard as I was. Her fingers squeezed me gently, and I almost came in my jeans. "Ailee, I need you." It was a desperate plea. Raw honesty. "Please, tell me you want to be with me, too."

I felt her head moving before I heard the words. "I do." A soft sound. Almost like a sob. "Tyler, I do."

"Where?"

I didn't need to explain my question. Raising her head, her blue eyes clashed with mine, and I wondered if I looked as strung out as I felt.

Ailee took my hand and led me back to her room. She started to close the door, but I stopped her, shaking my head. "Leave it." With the door open, a little light from the kitchen came in. Not too much, but just enough. Because when I took off her clothes—which I wanted to do as soon as possible—I wanted to see her. Every single womanly inch of her.

Before she could think too much about it, I turned her toward me. Eyes on her face, I gripped the bottom of her sweater and raised it, exposing the pale skin of her stomach. She lifted her arms, and I pulled it up and off. Her bra was blue and made out of some kind of smooth material. I cupped one of her breasts in my palm, feeling the weight, and felt her nipple harden beneath the pad of my thumb.

Ailee kicked off her shoes, and I did the same, then I grabbed the back of my shirt with one hand and pulled it over my head. I tossed it on the floor on top of hers. Without her shoes on, she barely came up to my shoulders.

Her eyes dropped to my chest, and I let her look. As much as I worked out for photo shoots, I still thought of myself as an average guy. But the way she was looking at me made me feel like I was one of those nude statues. A work of art to be admired.

Only with tats and a bigger dick.

She lifted her hand toward me, but paused midway, unsure.

"Go on," I told her. "Touch me, Ailee."

After a brief pause, she did, and I'd never felt anything fucking better. Her fingers were cold as they slid down the center of my chest, from my sternum to my stomach, then down to the waistband of my jeans. I let her explore, allowing her time to get more comfortable with my body.

Her tongue wet her bottom lip as her eyes followed the same trail, then dropped lower.

"Go ahead." I could barely get the words out, and I swallowed hard when her hands reached for the fastening of my jeans.

Unlike the frantic fumbling at the casino, in the privacy of her home, she took her time, unbuttoning my jeans and pulling the zipper down inch by slow inch.

Unable to wait anymore, I slid my hands inside my pants and pushed them down around my thighs until my cock was free, grabbing the condom out of my pocket as I did and throwing it on the bed. I'd never been so glad I'd thought to grab it. She wrapped her hand around me and squeezed, forcing a low moan from me, then dropped to her knees to finish what she'd started earlier.

This was not what I'd had in mind. But I made the mistake of looking down right as she took me in her mouth, and my knees nearly gave out at the combined sight and feel of Ailee giving me head. I slid my fingers into her hair and soaked it all in. The way the strands felt like silk as they cascaded over the backs of my hands. The wet heat of her mouth as she explored me. The sounds she made. The way her one hand gripped me near the base and the other held my hip, keeping me where I was so she could have her wicked way with me.

But mostly, the rush of desire in my blood and the sweet ache in my chest at this act of intimacy. I'd dreamed about it, fantasized about it, but none of it lived up to the reality of being here with this woman. A prisoner to her will.

My balls tightened. "Ailee." Her name was a moan, torn from me by the suction of her mouth. Holy fuck. I didn't want it to end this way. Ah, hell no. Not after I'd waited so long to be with her.

Gently, I pulled her away from me for the second time in one night. She looked up at me, and for a moment I couldn't move from the sight of her. Her lips were wet and swollen, her eyes blazing with lust, her skin flushed. I clenched my jaw and counted to ten, trying to think of the biggest asshole I knew in school. Brussel sprouts. Anything but this woman—but Ailee—looking at me like I'd just taken her favorite toy away.

I pulled her to her feet and kissed her hard, tasting myself on her tongue. She was still wearing her bra and her jeans, and I quickly set about divesting her of the remainder of her clothes. When she was bare to me, I stepped back, shaking my head when she tried to follow me.

Perfect.

She was fucking goddamned perfect.

Not that she didn't have what others would perceive as imperfections. She did. Her breasts were full, with areolas a few shades darker and rosier than her skin and tipped with dark pink nipples. They hung heavy, a little lower than younger girls. Her belly was slightly rounded, and yes, she had stretch marks and a long, horizontal scar from a surgery that left her a little saggy. Full hips curved around to highlight her pussy, then to thick thighs that gracefully tapered down to her ankles and feet. She had a body made for lovin'.

And I couldn't wait to do just that.

I yanked my jeans off, never taking my eyes from her. She stood awkwardly, a blush creeping up her chest and neck. I wondered if she would do that when I made her come. And I intended to find out. There was no reason at all for her to be self-conscious. "You're beautiful, Ailee," I told her. "God, so fucking beautiful."

Maybe it was the conviction in my voice. Maybe it was the hunger. Or the way I started to shake when I looked at her. But her blue eyes got wide and her shoulders went back. Now she stood before me, unashamed and full of confidence, and I'd never been so fucking turned on.

I took myself in my hand, trying to ease the ache there. Her eyes dropped down to watch, and her tongue shot out to wet her lips. I smiled at her, running my hand up and down my length as I stepped closer. Then I took her in my arms and kissed her quick and hard as I backed her up to the bed and laid her down.

She reached for me as I joined her, and for a brief second, I held myself above her, enjoying the anticipation. I felt the tips of her breasts brush my chest, then the soft curls between her thighs when she lifted her hips. I followed her back down, nestling between her legs.

Her soft curves cushioned my hardness perfectly. I actually got a little head rush when we came together.

She was soft and warm, her body moving restlessly beneath me. I kissed her again as I pushed my hips forward, sliding my length against her until I felt wet, silky heat.

Ailee moaned, and her nails dug into my back.

I worked my way down her neck, feeling her pulse flutter beneath my lips. Down over her collarbone to the valley between her breasts. I hefted one in my hand, bringing her nipple to my mouth. As I ran my tongue over her, it grew harder still, and I couldn't resist giving her a little nip with my teeth. She jumped a little, then groaned, grabbing my head and holding it where it was.

I moved to the other side and did the same thing, back and forth, until she was arching her back with her head back and her eyes closed. Then I started to move down, my palms sliding along her rib cage and hips. I kissed and tongued every line on her belly, dropping light kisses along the horizontal scar that ran from hip to hip.

Sitting back, I pushed her thighs apart. She gave the slightest resistance before giving in and opening to me, and I dropped onto my stomach between her legs. I ran my nose through the soft curls, smelling the earthy musk of her desire. An animalistic sound rumbled low in my throat, and I pushed her thighs wider, exposing her to my hungry eyes. She was plump and wet and ready.

I tasted her. Just the tip of my tongue to the smooth satin between her folds, tightening my hold on her.

Sweet. So fucking sweet.

Sliding my hands beneath her ass, I lifted her to my mouth. She shuddered in my hold, arching her back, grinding against my tongue even though I wanted to take it slow. I pushed my hips into the bed, fucking the mattress, the taste and feel of her so much more than I ever imagined. Ailee was such a woman. Earthy and real and passionate.

And she drove me fucking crazy.

With a moan, I explored her as she had me, finding and teasing the little hard nub before I gave her what she wanted. Her entire body tensed. Her moans as raw and lyrical as the music we'd danced to. Then she exploded around me in a great crescendo. I held her to my mouth, refusing to let her go as I helped her ride out her orgasm.

When she was nothing but a boneless mess on the bed, I rose over her and pressed the tip of my cock against her as I searched for that fucking condom. "Ailee?"

Her eyes opened, and her hands found my hips. She pulled me forward. "Yes, Tyler. Fuck me. Please."

With a groan, I ripped the package open with my teeth and rolled it on one-handed, then slid inside her, feeling her body squeeze me tight. She was so wet, cradling my hips like she was fucking made for me. "Oh God. Ailee..."

Suddenly, my head erupted into chaos. Voices filled the space, some shouting, some not. I froze, my head falling forward over her shoulder, as my hands slammed into my temples.

Not. NOW! The demand exploded through my head.

"Tyler?" She tried to lift my head up so she could see my face.

The voices were gone. But I was shaken.

What the FUCK was that?

I pulled out of her and sat up on the side of the bed. I was trembling uncontrollably. I was fucking scared.

Was I going crazy? What the hell was the matter with me?

"Tyler? Please. Talk to me. What's wrong? Did I do something?"

I wanted to reassure her. But I was too caught up in my own head. I felt around in there, scared shitless at what I might find.

But all was quiet.

Gradually, the room around me came back into focus. And I felt Ailee's hand on my back. I dropped my head into my hands. What the hell had just happened? And how was I supposed to explain without scaring her?

The air felt hot as the walls closed in on me. I couldn't breathe. I had to get the hell out of there.

Jumping up from the bed, I took off my only condom and started pulling on my clothes.

"Where are you going?"

I paused. What the fuck was I doing? She deserved better than this. But I had to get out of there. I was scared. Scared of what had just happened. Scared I would black out again. Scared I would hurt her or something else equally fucked up.

I turned to her with my pants undone and my shirt halfway on and took her face in my hands. "Ailee, you did nothing wrong. Do you hear me? Nothing. You are... you're fucking perfect. Don't ever doubt that. I just..." What? "I'm sorry. Something's going on with me. With my head. And I need to go." I kissed her hard and pulled my shirt the rest of the way on as I found my shoes.

She scrambled off the bed, searching for and finding her sweater. "What do you mean 'something with your head'?' Are you okay? Do you need to go to the hospital? I can take you."

Her concern pissed me off. I didn't deserve it. I was being an asshole, running out like this. But I didn't know how else to handle what was happening. I didn't know what else would happen, and it terrified the hell out of me. I didn't want her anywhere around this shit. "No. I just have to go." I paused at the bedroom door and took a long look at her.

She was sitting on the bed with her sweater on and her jeans in her hands, the white comforter a mess behind her. With her dark hair and white skin, she looked like a fairytale. "I'm so sorry."

Turns out I was no fucking prince.

CHAPTER 14

Ailee

I stood outside the apartment building in downtown Seattle. Butterflies jabbed their little antennae into the lining of my stomach, fluttering around in there trying to get out, and I almost lost my nerve and turned around.

I looked down at the paper in my hand. Tyler's address was written on it. I had it so I could send him his payment when he modeled for me. Was it an invasion of his privacy to use it this way? Bad business practice? Probably. Pretty certain it was, actually. But we were way beyond being nothing but business partners. We'd been naked together last night. Surely, that had to count for something. Right? Gave me some different privileges?

Plus, I was really worried about him. Obviously, he had some kind of health problem going on. It could be anything—migraines, a tumor. But whatever it was, I was the one who irritated it. Or rather, our physical attraction to each other. He'd run out on me twice now, and both times we'd been engaged in activities that really got the blood pumping.

I'm not sure how long I stood out there. A few people walked past me, some entering the apartment complex, some headed out to wander the city. Like my own building, there was an exterior door to enter the complex, and you needed a key or a code to get in. Unlike mine, it held none of that small-town charm, but was pale and nondescript. It was in a good location, though, close to public transit and a variety of stores.

I glanced at the number of his apartment on the paper again. It looked like his place was on the first floor. I took a deep breath. I couldn't just stand out here in the cold all day. Walking up to the door, I looked for some way to buzz Tyler, but before I could let him know I was here, the door opened and a young guy walked out. He held the door open for me, unconcerned about who was entering his building without access. Or, maybe I just didn't look threatening enough in my jeans and bright tangerine raincoat.

I smiled my thanks and hurried inside. Tyler's place was to the right and at the end of the hall. I rang the doorbell before I could second guess myself. Then I waited. A dog began to bark. Did he have a dog? I was about to pull a ding dong ditch when I heard him moving around inside.

The door opened, and Tyler stood there. He cocked his head and smiled at me with a pleasant expression on his face. "Hello," he said.

I frowned before I could stop myself. I could've sworn I'd just detected a trace of a European accent. He looked different. Softer. Swollen, maybe? "Hi," I told him. "I'm sorry for just showing up like this. I should've called or something. But I just wanted to check on you."

That pleasant smile faltered just a bit. He appeared confused.

"Your head?" I prompted, pointing at my own temple. "You ran out of my place the night before last? Said you had something going on with your head..." I trailed off, really scared now at the blank look in his eyes.

He facepalmed, a very un-Tyler-like move. "Yes, yes. Of course. Sorry, I've had a lot going on." He tilted his head to the side, like he was listening for something. Then he smiled. Stepping back, he made room for me to pass him. "Would you like to come in, Ailee?"

Tyler felt out my name on his tongue. Like he wasn't quite sure if that's who I was. Something weird was going on. This wasn't the Tyler I was getting to know, but it also wasn't the Tyler I'd seen at Whole Foods with his sister.

"Please, Ailee, come in." He held the door wider, my name spoken with more confidence that time.

I wasn't imagining it. Even his voice sounded different. I stood in the doorway, undecided if I should stay or leave. Obviously, he was fine. He was alive. He was home. And if he'd wanted to talk to me, he would've called me.

Maybe I should just go.

A little brown dog came bounding around the corner, ears and tongue flapping in the wind. He ran right out to me and jumped up on my legs, and my heart instantly overflowed, filling the hollowness that had been growing in the center of my chest. "Hey, buddy."

"Get down," Tyler told the dog. He pulled the little ball of excitement off of me and shooed him back into the apartment. "Sorry about that."

The dog hung his head and slunk off into another room.

That's it. I was going in. Just for a minute. "It's no problem," I told him as I stepped inside. "I love dogs." Hanging my jacket on the back of a chair, I set off in search of the pup, determined to cheer him up. Whatever Tyler's problem was with the dog, he needed to get over it.

I found him in the living room right off the kitchen, curled up in the corner. Sitting on the end of the couch near him, I patted my knee and invited him over to me. With a cautious look at Tyler, he crept out from his hidey-hole and sat at my feet. A few scratches behind his floppy ears was all it took to bring out his previous happy self. "So, why do you have a dog if you don't like them?"

Tyler perched on the other end of the couch. It was very big and very brown and distinctly masculine, and for some reason I couldn't put my finger on, he looked out of place sitting on the edge with his knees together and his hands on his lap. "I don't dislike dogs," he said. "I just try to get him to act like a gentleman when company comes over."

The flags I had folded and put away last night flew back up the flagpole and snapped to attention. If it had been said in the teasing manner I was coming to expect from Tyler, I would've laughed. But he wasn't teasing. Not at all. He was dead serious and sounded much like an uppity British woman.

What the hell was going on?

I turned my head, brushing my hair to the side so I could look at him. "Is this some kind of a game?" *Please tell me you're in a drama class and you're method acting or something. Because if you're not, this is too fucking weird.*

"Excuse me?" He pulled back, affronted.

"Why are you acting like this?" I gave the dog one last head rub and stood up. "Do you want me to leave? Because if that's the case, all you have to do is say so."

He stared at me for a long time. I fought not to fidget as I met his gaze with a challenge of my own and waited for him to respond.

Finally, he gave a little shake of his head. "No, Ailee. I don't want you to leave." He squinted, like his head was hurting, and rubbed his temples. "Look, I'm sorry I'm being weird, but I'm not ready to talk about it yet." He looked at me again, and I saw a flash of the man I knew in his expression. "Why don't you stay, and we can hang out. Do you have plans for today?"

I did, but nothing that couldn't be put off. So, I shook my head. "No. I don't have any plans. Not really." He had a tumor. That was the only explanation. At least, that's what I told myself. Anything else...well...I wasn't ready to think about that.

"I know Snickers would like it if you stayed."

"Is that his name?" I grinned down at the furry face that had been watching me with a forlorn expression since the moment I stood.

"Yes. There's a story behind it, but I think that's something for another time." He stood and clapped his hands together. "So, what do you say? I'll make some tea or some cocoa, and we can watch movies or something."

That actually sounded really nice, but I still had the feeling I was imposing somehow. "Don't feel like you have to invite me to stay just because I showed up here. Really. I just wanted to check on you, and you're obviously okay..." I trailed off as he approached me and took my hands.

"Ailee. I want you to stay. I want to get to know you better." He grinned. "And not in the biblical kind of way. Just...you." He gave me a little smile and shrugged.

I still wasn't completely comfortable, but I didn't feel threatened or anything. Just that something was off. And I wanted to figure out what it was. Something told me this wasn't just a game. "Okay. That sounds nice."

He smiled at me, his brown eyes warm and friendly.

It took me a minute to figure out what was different. And then I did. There was no heat in his gaze. Not one spark. Same as when I saw him at Whole Foods.

"Great. I'll go get our drinks."

As he walked away, I noticed for the first time what he was wearing. Soft, form-fitting pants clung to his muscular legs, and a long, baby-blue sweatshirt hung down past his hips.

Like something I would wear lounging around at home. Yeah, now that I thought about it, it *was* kind of feminine. But styles had changed quite a bit these days. Men didn't always wear stuff that was overtly masculine, and vice versa. And it wasn't unattractive on him.

"Tea or cocoa?" he asked from the kitchen.

"Tea," I replied. "Can I use your bathroom?"

"Of course. Down the hall. First door on your right."

I smiled at Snickers and told him I'd be right back, then made my way down the hall. I could see Tyler's room at the end, and with a peek over my shoulder, I wandered over to the doorway and looked in. A large bed took up most of the room. It had a dark leather backboard and was covered with a dark blue comforter. A small lamp and a thick book took up most of the space on the nightstand on the far side. On the wall closest to me looked to be the closet and maybe another bathroom.

Against the far wall, a wooden table was shoved into the corner. There were papers scattered across the top, drawings from the looks of it. I wanted to take a closer look, but I didn't feel comfortable just walking into his room.

I backtracked and quickly shut myself in the hall bathroom. It was only a half bath—a pedestal sink and a toilet—so there was nothing there to give me any insight into this man I was finding myself more and more entangled with. When I was finished, I washed my hands and headed back out to the living room. Snickers greeted me with a wagging tail and a smile.

I heard rain hitting the windows as Tyler came in with two mugs of tea. He set them on the coffee table and invited me to sit down. "What'll it be? A movie? A card game?"

I got comfy on the couch near Snickers. "How about Truth or Dare?"

Tyler sat near me, one leg tucked beneath him. He laughed at my suggestion. "Or...we could just talk."

"Okay." This was so strange. Sitting here with him now was kind of like hanging out with a new girlfriend for the first time. It was both weird and comfortable. I had no idea how he could turn it off and on again—that thing, whatever it was, that made the fire burn in my blood with nothing but a heated glance from him.

"So, you're divorced." He drew out the last word a bit.

"Yes." I was confused. "But you know that."

"I do." He sounded more confident this time. "Was it really bad?"

"The marriage or the divorce?"

He smiled. "Both."

"Um..." I wasn't sure where he was going with this. "We already talked about a lot of this the other night. Don't you remember?"

He stared at me hard, but I had the strangest feeling he wasn't seeing me at all. After a few seconds, he focused on my face. "That's right. We did."

I picked up my tea and took a sip. It was good. Some kind of orange spice. "It was the best thing I ever did."

"What about before," he said.

"Before?"

"Before you got married. Or even thought about marriage. What did you want to do with your life?"

"Well, like most girls, I wanted to be a ballerina when I was like, six." I laughed. "Of course, it would've helped if I'd actually taken lessons."

He laughed a little, nodding in agreement.

"When I met my ex, I was actually pursuing a business degree..."

We ended up hanging out all afternoon. Two movies and hours of conversation later, I told him I had to go. "This was fun, Tyler." And it had been. Strange, but fun. I felt like I'd just made a new friend, and I couldn't explain why.

At the door, I waved to Snickers, suddenly unsure. I wanted to kiss Tyler goodbye, and yet, I didn't.

Tyler solved the problem by leaning down and giving me a chaste kiss on the cheek. "I'll see you soon. Thank you for coming over to check on me. I had fun today."

"Me, too." With a final wave at Snickers, I smiled and left.

The temperature had dropped, but luckily the rain had let up to barely a drizzle. I wandered the streets of the city, my head lost in thought. I was scared for Tyler.

Something was obviously wrong with him, but I understood if he didn't want to talk about it. Maybe he was waiting for test results or something.

It suddenly occurred to me that not once during our entire afternoon together, or any other time we'd spent together, had he mentioned family or friends. Other than a brief mention of his foster parents and his sister. And he hadn't mentioned her at all today.

If he was dealing with something health-wise, he would need a good support system. People to help him get to appointments, sit with him, maybe worse. And I didn't have time for that shit.

Shame quickly followed. How could I think that way? I mean, seriously, how fucking selfish could I be?

I stopped in the middle of the street and looked around. Tears filled my eyes, blurring the sight of the city just beginning to light up for the night. I didn't even know what I was crying about. For Tyler? Or for myself?

But I did know. I wasn't crying because I was selfish. I was crying because he'd made me care. And now I didn't know what the hell was going to happen to him. I didn't even know where he'd gone today. Because that may have been Tyler's body sitting next to me, but it sure as hell wasn't Tyler.

Wiping the moisture from my eyes, I realized I wasn't far from Stef's apartment. I thought about stopping by, but honestly, I wouldn't be great company, and I had to catch the bus back home. Taking a deep breath, I crossed the street and headed toward the bus stop. I had a full day at the studio tomorrow. For right now, I would think about that and only that.

And I was a fool if I believed I could do that.

CHAPTER 15

Tyler

Squinting against the bright sunlight, I rolled over to look at the clock...

And fell from the couch onto the floor, banging my head on the edge of the coffee table. "Fuckin' hell!" The words were thick on my tongue. On my hands and knees, I raised my head and stared at the two empty mugs in front of me. There was a bowl shoved off to the side with a few popcorn kernels left in the bottom.

I groaned as my head throbbed like I'd just gotten off of a three-week bender. "What the fuck?"

A long tongue licked a wet trail up my face and I closed my eyes again before it jabbed my eyeball and reached for my dog. "Hey, buddy." The sense of panic that had been swiftly rising within me subsided as I received the best good morning a guy could get, other than if Ailee was here, maybe.

I eyed the mugs again. *Had* she been here? Did she even know where I live? I guess she would, being she was the one who sent me my checks. Willow was the only other person who came by on the regular, and she was a caffeine junkie through and through. Coffee only for that girl. The stronger, the better.

Snickers let out a yip and jumped up to lick me again. "All right, all right. Whatcha need, buddy?" I got up and headed into the kitchen to check his food and water.

But he had other plans. The pup half ran, half skidded to the back door and did a little dance, his nails clicking on the tiles.

"Ah, I get it." I opened the patio door for him, leaving it open so he could come back in when he was ready.

My phone was lying on the counter, and I picked it up. The battery was down to five percent, and I had two missed calls from Ailee and a text message from my sister. I glanced at the screen again as I walked back to my room. Was it too early to call Ailee back?

It was eight in the morning, on Wednesday, September 18th.

Wednesday.

I stopped just inside my room. That couldn't be right. If it was, I'd missed the first day of classes. The last thing I remembered was leaving Ailee's place on Friday night.

What had I done after I'd left? On legs stiff from being crunched up on the couch, I hobbled to the bed and sat down as I tried to figure out why this was happening again. In some distant recess of my brain, it occurred to me that it had been made. I never made my bed. Didn't see the point. My heart began to pound so hard I thought it was gonna break through my ribcage and my head felt light. The world spun around me, and I forced myself to breathe.

Just breathe.

Closing my eyes, I concentrated on each inhale and exhale. When I opened them again, I was staring at my lap...

At a baby blue shirt I didn't remember owning, and pants that were way too tight on my legs.

I jumped up from the bed, still staring down at myself. "What the actual fuck??" Tearing off the sweatshirt, I rounded the bed to get another one from my dresser—one I would fucking remember wearing—and came up short at the sight of a table beneath the window.

Slowly, I approached it, almost afraid of what I would find.

It was covered with drawings. Pictures of rooms and furniture and fireplaces, all different versions of the same room. Looking closer, I realized these were all drawings of my living room, with the furniture rearranged and with different decor. Yeah. There was the big window, and the shape of the room was exactly the same.

Dropping the drawing in my hand, I backed away from the table. I didn't even know how the fuck the thing had gotten in here.

Okay. Okay. Stay cool. It's okay. But it wasn't okay. It wasn't fucking okay at all.

I picked up the sweatshirt from where I'd dropped it on the floor and pulled off the pants, dropping them both into the corner near the laundry basket. I wasn't wearing any underwear. Naked, I strode across my room and straight into the shower. By the time I came out, I was a little bit calmer.

I needed to go see a doctor. There was no denying it anymore. The appointment I'd told Ailee about had gotten cancelled and I never rescheduled it. I think I was too afraid. But I couldn't keep running from this. Something was seriously wrong with me. And it wasn't a drinking problem. I had no alcohol in my apartment. I'd had a few glasses of wine with Ailee, but that was nowhere near enough to cause blackouts that lasted for days. And I don't think I'd hit the bars after leaving her place, if any had even been open that late. Mostly because I'd made it home and hadn't woken up behind a Dumpster or worse.

Still naked, I found my phone on the bed and plugged it in, then I threw on some jeans and a black T-shirt and grabbed my laptop from the floor where it was charging. I didn't know why it was there. I usually kept it in the living room. But at this point, I wasn't questioning it. I'd drive myself fucking insane.

With a small shake of my head, I sat on the bed and flipped it open. There was no password needed to log on, and I was grateful, because I don't think I could've remembered it for the life of me. I found the website I had bookmarked months ago when I'd first realized this shit was happening to me. Someone different from my regular doctor. Unlike then, I actually made an emergency appointment for later that same day.

Four hours later, I walked into the new doctor's office. Studying my previous records, he quickly ruled out any kind of physical problem, and I was shuffled straight to the office of a counselor who specialized in trauma. Two hours after that, I was heading home. But I had another appointment the next day with a therapist the counselor knew and recommended.

I called Ailee while I waited for the bus. She didn't answer, and I was glad. I wasn't sure I could sound normal if I spoke to her directly. I left her a message, telling her I had to go out of town for a while to help my folks, and I'd call her as soon as I could. I had no idea when that would be, but it was the best I could come up with. I didn't know yet what was going on with me, but I did know there was *something*.

For the first time in a long time, I felt a glimmer of hope alongside the fear.

In the few hours I'd talked to the counselor, I'd figured out that it probably wasn't a great idea to drag Ailee into all of this. This was my problem, not hers. However, I wasn't willing to give her up. Not now. Not when fate had given me this chance with her.

But right now, I had to take care of me. And all I could do was hope she would still be around when I came out of this.

Five Weeks Later

I had a diagnosis. Or at least, what my therapist and I thought was a diagnosis. Mostly thanks to my sister, who'd finally opened up to me about a lot of stuff.

After three weeks of getting a whole lot of nowhere, I'd called Willow and invited her over. Mostly because she wouldn't stop blowing up my phone.

She didn't react at all when I told her I was going to therapy, which was kind of odd. But when I shared all the things that had been happening to me and how freaked out I was by it, she started to cry.

"I'm so sorry, Tyler." She folded into one of the kitchen chairs, her thin hands covering her face.

I sat down, turning my chair toward her. "It's not your fault I'm fucked up, Will. We don't know where I came from, or what genetics I'm carrying." I gave a derisive laugh. "But now we know maybe why my biological parents didn't want me."

She was shaking her head even as she wiped her eyes. "That's not true." With a sniff, she grabbed my hand in both of hers and held it on her lap. "Mom and Dad know where you came from. I overheard them talking one night when we were teenagers."

The world stilled around me as I tried to comprehend what she was telling me. "What? How...how could they know?" And then a thought occurred to me. "This is why I was never adopted. Wasn't it?"

Horror crossed her face. "No! No, Tyler. This has nothing to do with that."

I didn't believe her, and she knew it.

"Tyler, I wasn't adopted, either. Mom and Dad have their reasons, the major one probably being money. I don't really know all of it. But I do know they love you, and not adopting you had nothing at all to do with where you came from."

"And where is that, exactly?"

Still holding my hand, Willow leaned forward, wisps of her blond hair falling over her thin shoulders, her eyes huge in her pale face. "I don't know what country or city exactly. I didn't hear that part. But it's somewhere in the Middle East. You were removed from a country at war." She gave me a sad smile. "I think your biological parents died."

They were dead. The word reverberated through me. My family, my mother who gave birth to me, was dead. And that was the exact moment I knew that I'd always had it in the back of my mind that I would meet her someday. A day that would never come now. "Why didn't you tell me?"

"You used to have nightmares when they first brought you home. You'd wake up terrified in your bed, screaming in terror most of the time." Her thumb rubbed the back of my hand in a soothing motion. "Do you remember coming in to sleep with me?"

I shook my head, trying to grasp what she was saying. I didn't remember any of this.

She glanced down at our joined hands. "You did it a lot at first. I think you felt safer with me for some reason. Maybe because I was another kid? You didn't speak much English, so you couldn't understand a lot of what was being said when Mom and Dad would come rushing into your room. I think it just scared you even more." She looked up at me and shrugged. "It made Mom pretty sad that you wouldn't let her comfort you."

"I don't remember any of that."

"That doesn't surprise me." Her eyes filled again. "It was horrible, Tyler. Hearing you scream like that."

"I'm so sorry, Willow."

But she waved away my apology. "Oh, honey. It's not your fault. I mean, hell. You were still healing from injuries when we first got you. Mom and Dad had to take you to the doctor all the time." She paused. "But I'm getting off track."

I laughed without humor, using the heel of one hand to wipe at the moisture in my eyes. Willow still held the other. "There's more to this fucking story?"

"Yeah. And before I start, please remember that I was only trying to protect you. That was always my intention, Tyler. I love you so much, and I just wanted it all to go away. I didn't want you to be scared anymore. I wanted you to be happy."

Well, I was really fucking scared now. But as I studied my sister's face, I saw that she truly meant it. So, I tried to keep the tremble from my voice when I asked, "What else, Willow?"

She took a deep breath. "A few months after you came to live with us, you woke me up one night like you did all the time. Only you weren't scared, Tyler, or even upset. Actually, you were happy."

"Well, that's good. Right?" I tried a smile. She didn't return it. A hollow feeling filled my chest. "Willow?"

She looked right at me then. "You told me your name was Superman."

I frowned. I didn't see what she was getting at. "Okay. So what? Kids pretend all the time. And I was like, what? Four? Five?"

"That's what I thought, too. I thought you were finally starting to play. You would 'pretend' to be Superman pretty often. Especially when something upset you or when the dreams got bad. I always passed it off as a kid being a kid. Mom and Dad never seemed concerned about it, either. At least, not in front of me. You were in school, you were picking up English like crazy, and you even played with some of the kids at recess. And eventually, Superman stopped coming around."

I frowned at her. I still didn't know where she was going, reliving the past like this. Other than the fact of where I came from. "So, you're saying you think I have PTSD or something? From when I was a kid?"

"I think it's more than that, Ty."

"Yeah, well, you're not a shrink. So..." I don't know why I suddenly felt defensive.

Just tell her to go. We don't need her.

I shook my head. Where the hell had that come from?

"Tyler? You okay?"

I focused on Willow. "Yeah, I'm fine. What are you trying to tell me?"

"Tyler, years later, after we'd both moved to Seattle, I stopped over to tell you about my shitty boss at that job I had. Remember that job?"

"I remember."

"When I came to your apartment, I met Tony." She waited for my reaction.

I racked my brain, trying to figure out who the hell she was talking about. I didn't remember knowing anyone named Tony. "I don't know anyone named Tony. Are you sure you met him here?"

"Tony was you, Ty. *You* told me you were Tony."

My heart began to pound. "What?"

"He's a little rough around the edges, quite honestly. I think he's there to protect you. But, anyway, I was sitting here talking to you—talking to him—when I had an idea. I asked him if he knew Superman."

Shoving my chair back, I stood up fast. "What the hell are you talking about? I'm not five anymore. I don't play games like that."

She went on as if I hadn't interrupted her, a determined set to her jaw and worry in her eyes. "He said he did, but that Superman didn't like to leave anymore. He just stayed in and played." She paused. "Tony's a little bit scary, but he seemed okay with me being here. He's a boxer and spends a lot of time at the gym. He also loves nothing more than watching *Mash* reruns." She grinned, even though her voice was thick with tears. "Where do you think you get all those muscles from?"

No. This was a bunch of bullshit. Why the fuck was she telling me this shit? I started pacing around my small kitchen. "If that's true, why don't I ever find gym clothes lying around?"

"I don't know. I guess you—he—changes at the gym before you come home."

"Stop saying that, Willow. He's not a real person." But there was *something*...something inside...that felt seen. It was all starting to click. I stopped on the other side of the table and gripped the back of a chair. I felt ridiculous even asking this question. "Does Tony like to drink, by chance?"

She gave a little shake of her head. "I don't know."

Pushing away from the table, I turned my back to her, trying to process the fuck ton of emotions whipping around inside of me. But the biggest one—the *biggest* one —made me stop, close my eyes, and drop my head back on my neck. Because it was fucking relief. "So, I'm like my own version of Jekyll and Hyde." I laughed out loud. It was an ugly sound. "What the fuck, Willow?" I whispered as the tears returned.

Her arms wrapped around me from behind. "I'm so sorry, Tyler. I should've told you. I should've made you go to a doctor years ago. But I was scared they would lock you up somewhere. And honestly, Tony wasn't that bad. Once he decided to like me, we hung out once or twice. I haven't seen him in a while, but you've been kind of unavailable lately."

"He's been around," I muttered. I held her arms tight around me. "So, what? I have multiple personalities or something?"

"I think...maybe."

"Fuck." The word was no more than a whisper. What the hell was I supposed to do with this? "Superman and Tony. You'd think I'd pick cooler names." I'd meant it as a joke, but I couldn't bring myself to laugh.

"And Miko," she mumbled into my back. "He's kind of fun. We went grocery shopping once." She held on tighter. "Ailee met him, too."

This time, I did laugh. I laughed until tears ran down my face and I wouldn't have been able to stay standing if it weren't for my sister holding me up. I laughed until I cried. Until sobs tore from my chest and we both ended up in some kind of twisted puddle on the floor. Willow refused to let me go even then.

"Tyler, it's okay. It will be okay. I'm so sorry. I should have told you, but I thought they would go away like Superman did. I thought if I just watched out for you, it would all go away. You would be okay."

I could barely understand her. She was crying nearly as hard as I was.

We stayed like that—my sister and I—on the floor in my kitchen, for a long, long time. When we could, we got up, got a notebook, and began to write it all down so I could take it to my therapist. Willow wanted to call our parents, but I didn't want to tell them anything just yet.

Two weeks later, I called Ailee and told her I was back in town.

CHAPTER 16

Ailee

I looked around at the pile of clothes I'd thrown on the floor of my closet in the last hour. There had to be something there that was suitable for a "first time you're seeing your boyfriend in two months" date.

Was it a date? I assumed it was a date. But maybe boyfriend was a strong word. Although, the last time I'd seen Tyler was our movie day, and that sure as hell had not felt like a date. Nothing at all like our night at the casino, which had been nothing but hours of foreplay.

I pressed the heels of my hands to my forehead. What if it wasn't a date? What if this was a "Hey, I'm back but only to pack my stuff because I'm moving home and it was nice knowing ya" kind of thing?

Oh God, I had no idea what to wear for that.

Glancing out the door at the clock on my nightstand, I cursed. Tyler would be here in ten minutes. I took a deep breath. Well, if he was going to break up with me, I was damn well going to be comfortable while I drowned my sorrows in the half gallon of ice cream I'd picked up earlier. Just in case.

Black yoga pants and a long-sleeved, baby-blue thermal shirt, it was. Fuzzy socks completed the outfit. I figured it was my best bet. Yoga pants were both comfy and sexy, so that could go either way. I brushed my hair and left it loose. It was getting long and hung well past my shoulders. I'd put on minimal makeup after my shower. Didn't want mascara running my cheeks. That was not a good look on me. I knew this from previous experience.

Oh, God. I wasn't ready for him to break up with me. Dammit.

Dressed and ready, I wandered out to the kitchen to make some tea. The silence in my apartment was deafening, so I set my phone down by my little kitchen speaker and turned on some music. *Trouble* by Halsey was playing on Spotify, and I almost laughed at how perfectly it suited this exact moment. With a tap on my phone screen, I put it on repeat.

My stomach growled in protest at my spontaneous fasting, but I didn't think I'd be able to eat. I'd been in knots since Tyler had called the night before, asking if he could come over and see me. I hadn't even known he was back in town, and he'd just texted me the day before that.

I resisted the urge to rub my tired eyes as I tried to recall if he'd said anything about it, but I was positive he hadn't. While he was gone, he'd called me about once a week, and texted almost every day, but mostly we'd chatted about a whole lot of nothing. Other than saying he was helping his foster dad out with his business, a business I still knew nothing about, we spent most of our conversations talking about me and what I was doing and who I was shooting that week. I told him about an opportunity that had come up to have my photos in a local magazine, and how my daughter had called to invite me to come see her over the holidays.

For the most part, it had all been very civil and friendly and not at all like the fiery man I'd come to know. Yet, on occasion, he would tell me that he missed me, his voice raw and full of need. And in those moments, I caught glimpses of the Tyler I knew, and the connection between us was still there. Rare, but real.

Three soft knocks on my door had my heart pounding. I stared at it for a moment, frozen, afraid. It took a few seconds before I convinced my feet to move. I slid the deadbolt, turned the knob, and opened the door wide.

Tyler stood there looking like sin in a gray skull cap, a fitted black jacket, black jeans and boots. His hands were in his pockets and his eyes were black in the dim lighting of the hallway, yet they burned me alive as they swept over my face and down my body.

Blood rushed to my nether regions so fast I got lightheaded.

Oh, God.

"Can I come in?" he asked. "I need to come in, Ailee. Please."

I realized I was blocking the doorway and quickly stepped back. "Of course. Come in."

With one powerful step, he was inside with the door closed and sweeping me up into his arms. "I missed you so much."

My arms went around his neck. *Oh God.* I'd missed him, too. More than I'd realized until just this very moment. "I missed you, too." He smelled like soap and something woodsy and masculine. I wanted to crawl inside his clothes with him. Emotions welled up inside of me. Emotions I hadn't felt for a man in...well, never. They were real and obsessive and raw, and too much. It was all too much.

"I'm so sorry I took off like that." Taking my face between his large palms, his eyes bored into mine. "I never meant to be gone so long."

I tried to play it cool. "That's okay. Things come up. You did what you had to do."

One side of his mouth turned up in response. His eyes travelled over my face. "I almost forgot how pretty you are."

Tears filled my eyes, but before he could notice, he was kissing me.

My hands gripped the front of his coat and I hung on for all I was worth, praying my knees wouldn't give out. How was this happening? How had I ended up here? Clinging to a man like he was my lifeline. This wasn't what I wanted.

Before I could go any farther down that trail of thought, I was spun around and my back was up against the door.

Tyler broke off the kiss and stepped back just far enough to rip his coat from his body, revealing a gray T-shirt pulled tight across his muscular chest. His eyes never left my face, my mouth, dipping down to my breasts. And then he was against me, one hand in my hair and his mouth slamming down on mine. I moaned at the warmth of his body. The taste of him. The delicious scent of him. The strength of his arms around me. The hard press of his body.

God, I wanted him. I couldn't deny it. The entire time he'd been gone, I'd walked around in a fog, going through the motions of my life, and yet never really feeling alive.

Tyler made me feel alive. And I craved this feeling like a drug.

My hands went to the bottom of his shirt and started wriggling it up and off. He growled low in his throat when it forced him to release me. I pushed the hat off his head and dropped it. His dark hair stuck up all over, and it was so damn sexy.

"I missed you," I told him again, and I meant it. I missed this Tyler. This man who looked at me like he hungered for me more than air, who touched me like he couldn't get close enough, and made me feel like the only woman on earth. Or, at least, the only woman for him. I don't know where he'd gone after our date at the casino, but I'd missed him so damn much.

He cupped my cheek tenderly, even as he pressed his hard length against my stomach. "Ailee," he whispered. "We need to talk."

"I'd rather do what we're doing," I told him. My hands roved over his hard body. Over the tattoos on one side of his chest and upper arms. Whatever he wanted to talk about could wait. I needed this reconnection with him. I wanted to finish what we'd started at my apartment.

"Ailee..." His expression was pained.

I took off my shirt and dropped it on the new pile of clothes we were creating. "After," I whispered. "Please, kiss me now."

With a helpless sound, he did. Gently at first, his lips brushing the corners of my mouth, playing with my bottom lip, leaving a trail of heat along my jawline before returning to my mouth. Gathering my hair back into one hand, he pulled, tilting my head back so he could leave wet kisses down my throat.

He slid his other hand over my ass, squeezed, then went lower, brushing my core from behind with his fingertips and pulling one leg up to wrap around his hip. He lifted me easily, my other leg wrapping around him as he balanced me against the door. Bolts of desire shot all the way through to my limbs when he rolled his hips. He was so hard, so strong, I could barely breathe for wanting him.

Still holding me wrapped around him, he jerked me up into him and took me to my room. I felt a brief jolt of fear he was going to run out on me again, but it was gone by the time he sat on the side of the bed with me on his lap. Reaching around me, he undid his boots one at a time and kicked them off. And then his mouth was on me again, leaving wet heat everywhere he touched.

His thumb brushed the underside of my breast, and I pushed him back onto the bed. He laid back, watching me as I unhooked my bra and slid the straps down my arms. His eyes latched onto my chest and his breath stopped as my breasts were freed. Catching them in his hands, he squeezed my nipples, rolling them between his fingers.

My head fell back, and I arched my spine, shamelessly pushing harder into his palms as I moved my hips, rubbing against his hard length. I needed him inside of me. I needed him with me. This woman I became when I was with him, I didn't know where she came from, but I really liked her. She wasn't shy. Wasn't ashamed of her body. She held the power, even as he played her like an instrument and made her weak with need.

With a growl, he sat up and took a nipple in his mouth. I held onto his strong shoulders, watching him. There was a flash of white teeth as he nipped at me, then pulled me closer, sucking the hard nub into his mouth as he teased it with his tongue. One hand slid down the back of my pants, gripping my bare ass. The other arm held me prisoner to him.

I'd never felt as sexy as I did when I was in Tyler's arms.

With a surge of strength, he flipped me over onto my back on the bed. The power in his body was nothing short of amazing. He stood above me, his eyes roving over my half nude form before he bent down with a show of rippling abs and began pulling off my yoga pants. I wore nothing beneath.

When my pants joined the rest of our clothes on the floor, he undid his jeans and shoved them and his boxer briefs down over his lean hips and muscular legs. I couldn't take my eyes off him. He was beautiful, like a wild animal was beautiful. Sleek and powerful and fully aroused.

He took himself in his hand as he watched me, biting his bottom lip. "Don't move," he ordered. "I just want to look at you for a minute."

I felt heat creep up my chest and neck, but I forced myself to lie still as he grabbed a condom from his jeans and rolled it on. He didn't touch me, but he didn't need to. I was about to come just from the intensity of his stare and the raw need vibrating from his body.

"You're so fucking beautiful, Ailee." His voice was full of what I could only call wonder. "So fucking perfect for me." A shadow of pain crossed his face, and he shook his head slightly. His lips moved, saying something I couldn't hear, but then he was lifting me higher into the bed and his weight was pressing me down into the mattress. My body cradled his perfectly as he kissed me hard.

"I'm sorry," he whispered against my lips. And then he was sliding inside of me, pushing deep, filling me.

I wanted to tell him he didn't need to apologize; I was more than ready. But he was moving, pumping in and out with long, hard strokes, one hand beneath my hips to lift me to him and an elbow braced beside my head. His eyes met mine and held me, more intimately than our bodies.

A sob rose in my throat. I was so overwhelmed with it all, like our souls were touching.

"Is this real?" he whispered. I saw a flash of fear, and I held him tighter, but he pulled away from me.

"No!" I called out before I stop myself.

But he just smiled and crawled down my body, taking me with his mouth.

I cried out, my hands fisting the blankets as my orgasm hit me hard and fast. Tyler groaned—a sexy sound of masculine satisfaction—as he devoured me with his tongue and lips and teeth, biting the inside of my thigh before surging over me and pushing inside as my muscles contracted around him, squeezing, holding him tight within me.

His hands wrapped around my wrists, holding them above my head as he shifted over me until he was hitting my clit with every thrust. "Ailee." My name was a moan of pleasure. "Come for me again, sweetheart. Come with me."

I lost my breath as my body responded to his words. He swelled inside of me as he gave in to his own needs, pounding into me, my cries mixing with his own as I felt the waves of another orgasm building, higher and higher, until they crashed over the edge, my body convulsing hard beneath him as he pushed deep, his head dropping to my shoulder, his body shuddering over me.

We stayed like that as we caught our breath. Then he released my wrists and rolled off of me, pulling me on top of him and cradling my head against his chest.

Neither of us spoke as he played with my hair, spreading it across his bare skin and rubbing the ends between his fingers. I didn't want to move. Didn't want to ruin this moment. Didn't want to hear what he had to say.

My nervousness from earlier returned in a sudden rush.

"Ailee, we need to talk."

I stilled, buried my nose in the warmth of his skin and inhaled deep, pulling his scent deep into me. Maybe it was better to get it over with. Rip off the Band-Aid. "Okay," I said into his chest.

"Let's go get some tea, and we can talk in the kitchen."

I stiffened. This wasn't good. Oh, my God. He *was* dying. Or moving. Or leaving me forever in some shape or form. With a reluctant sigh, I moved off of him.

Just as reluctantly, he let me go.

Tyler pulled on his jeans as I went into the bathroom to clean up. When I came out, he was gone, so I threw on my long shirt and joined him in the kitchen. He was shirtless and barefoot at the stove, turning on the burner beneath the teakettle when I walked in. He eyed my shirt for a second, his face carefully blank, before he came over and took my hand. Turning it over, he kissed the center of my palm, then brushed the hair from my face. His eyes softened for a moment as he looked at me.

"So, why don't you just lay it on me," I blurted out. "I can't stand the suspense anymore. Although," I quickly got in before he could say anything. "I'd just like to put it out there that I really fucking hate you for making me care if you're just going to leave me."

His eyebrows rose in surprise. "What? Who said I was leaving you?"

"Aren't you?" If he wasn't leaving me, then why were his shoulders so stiff and little worry lines creasing his forehead?

"No, sweetheart. Not unless you make me go." The tea kettle whistled. He ignored it, dropping his head to brush his lips against mine. Then, with a sigh, he finally said, "Want to sit and I'll get our tea?"

Grateful I didn't have to depend on my legs anymore to hold me up, I dropped into the nearest chair and waited for Tyler to join me. My mind was racing, thinking up every worst-case scenario I could imagine. I took a breath and steeled myself. All I could do was wait for him to fill me in.

He joined me at the table, setting a cup in front of me. Steam rose from the surface and I pulled it to me, inhaling the sweet notes of rooibos and cinnamon. Halsey was still playing over the speaker. I should go shut it off, or at least take it off repeat.

Tyler cleared his throat. "So, first. I need to come clean about something."

Shit. Here it comes. I never should've gotten involved with a younger guy. I knew it. As mature as he normally came across, he still had oats to sew. Why didn't I listen to me?

"I wasn't out of town all this time. I've been here, in Seattle. And I'm so sorry I lied to you about that. I just needed some time."

Okay. That wasn't so bad. "Time for what?" I don't know why I asked, because I wasn't sure I really wanted to know.

He took a sip of his tea, then pressed his lips together for a moment before telling me, "As you kinda know, I've been having some…I don't know…episodes? Some even worse than what you've seen." He paused. "Ailee, I've been having blackouts. Sometimes for days."

I held myself very still. "Blackouts? From what?" It was a tumor. I knew it.

He tried to laugh, but it was more a burst of frustration. "I don't fucking know. For a while, I thought I was some kind of closet alcoholic, waking up behind Dumpsters and on other people's couches. I just never remembered actually starting to drink. I couldn't remember where I'd been. What I'd done." His eyes met mine. "I'd just get up, get back to life, and try to forget that it ever happened because, honestly, it freaked me the hell out. And each time I'd just hope and pray it wouldn't happen again…

"But now there are things going on in my life. Good things. Fucking great things." A sweet smile curled his lips as he looked at me. "And after seeing you again…" His eyes darkened. "I wanted you the first time we met, Ailee. I still want you. Even now, my heart is pounding in my fucking chest just looking at you."

I had no doubt it was true. I could see it in his eyes, black as night. My breath caught as my stomach flipped over. I still wasn't used to such intense declarations.

"But even after we started seeing each other, I tried to ignore it, hoping somehow things would get back to normal, but it didn't. And I was scared, Ailee. So fucking scared." Fear tightened his features.

I reached out to him, touching his hand.

"I'm not a fucking alcoholic. I knew it then and I know it now. But something was going on with me, and I knew I needed to get a grip on this if I was going to be any good at all for you, so I went to see my doctor, which led to me being referred to a therapist."

"A therapist? For what?" Relief made me weak. I'd really thought he was dying. Therapy, I could handle. Maybe he had anxiety or something.

"We think I have Dissociative Identity Disorder. DID." The words rushed out, like he was afraid if he didn't just get them out there, he would never be able to say them.

Everything stilled around me. Over the sound of the music, I heard raindrops hitting the window. One of the neighbors closed their door, jingling their keys. The clock on the stove ticked. Before the blood rushed through my ears, muting it all behind a wall of disbelief.

Tyler chewed his lower lip, studying me closely for my reaction. When I didn't say anything, he continued. "It's caused by a severe trauma that happens in childhood. Um..." He squinted one eye like his head hurt. "I don't know what that trauma was; I can't remember. It's something we're working on. But whatever it was that happened to me, it was enough that my brain needed to protect me from it to survive. To do that, it created other people—alters—to handle what I couldn't. Basically. Do you know what I mean? I feel like I'm making no fucking sense." He put his elbows on the table and rubbed his temples.

He was explaining himself well enough. Pictures of him as a young child with big, brown eyes and shaggy, dark hair came to mind, and my heart splintered in my chest at the thought of that child enduring something so horrific that his body took over and protected him the only way it could. I'd taken my share of Psych classes. I knew exactly how horrific those experiences had to have been. Had he been abused?

Tyler's face blurred before me, and I felt wetness on my cheeks. "You have multiple personalities?"

With a small shrug, he said, "Yeah. I guess. They weren't sure at first. It's still early days with the therapy."

"Then why do you think that?" A small glimmer of hope sparked in my chest. Maybe it wasn't DID. Maybe it was something less...life-altering.

"Well, mostly because Willow told me she's met a few of them. The alters."

I went numb. Well, for the most part. My heart broke for him, and for me. Scenes from movies played in my head, characters with multiple personalities—or what did he call them? Alters?—going psycho and killing people. A flash of fear shot through me. I sat back in my chair, staring at this man I thought I was coming to know. What the hell had I gotten myself into?

"Don't look at me like that, Ailee."

I averted my eyes, but like a car accident, I couldn't stop myself from looking and they kept going back to him. I watched his expression, the way his fingers tapped the tabletop, much like he had at the coffee shop that first time. Wild thoughts buzzed through my head. Who was this I was talking to? Who is the real Tyler? Is it even Tyler, or is this man one of the alters who'd taken over the physical body? Would he hurt me? What if he switched right now? Right here?

"Fuck, 'lee. I'm not going to murder you in your kitchen."

"How do you know that?"

He opened his mouth to reply, but snapped it closed again. His head fell forward, and my heart jumped in my chest, but when he raised it again, it was still Tyler staring out at me. And his face was twisted with his emotions. "I'm sorry, Ailee. I'm so fucking sorry. I wanted to tell you what was going on from the start, but I wanted to have something to actually tell you first, other than the fact that I've woken up in strange places more than a few times only to find out days have gone by. Days I don't fucking remember. Chunks of my life gone. Just fucking gone!" He paused. Took a breath. "I wanted to tell you as soon as I got here. I didn't mean for us to..." He stopped. "I just missed you so fucking much."

"Were you covered in blood?" I shouldn't have said that. But I couldn't stop myself. "Did you have blood on you any of those times you woke up?"

"What? No, Ailee." Hurt and confusion lit his eyes as he drew back from me.

God, what was I doing. I covered my face with my hands. "I'm sorry. I shouldn't have said that. That wasn't fair of me. It's just..." And suddenly, it all came crashing down. The day I'd seen him with his sister at Whole Foods. The last time I'd seen him.

"What? What is it?"

"It's all starting to make sense. The store." Our movie day. I almost slapped my hand to my forehead. "I came to your apartment—"

His stare bore into me. "When?"

"A few days after you ran out on me. I was worried about you and stopped by to see you. You hadn't called or texted..." I trailed off. "We talked and watched movies." I looked up at him. "That wasn't you, was it?"

He stared at me. His shoulders fell, all of the fight leaving him. "I don't remember that. I'm so sorry."

Oh, my God. That explained so much. "Who was I with all day, Tyler?"

He shrugged. "I don't know."

I looked away. I wasn't sure how to feel about all of this.

"I told my therapist about you. That you were in my life. And I'm really hoping that's not going to change."

I stared down into my tea, lost in my own thoughts. I didn't say anything. I couldn't.

"I get it. It's a lot to take on."

The careful control he kept to his voice tore at me. "What happened to you?" I cried softly. "To cause this?" The fact that it was real, I had no doubt. I'd met one, maybe two, of his alters. I knew I had. That was why the connection between us wasn't there, the raw need. Because it wasn't fucking him.

"I'm not sure. Willow says I was born in a country at war. Apparently, my biological parents were both killed there. When I was brought here, I had sustained some kind of injuries." He rubbed his forehead again. "I need to call my parents and ask them, I guess."

"You haven't talked to them?"

He shook his head. "Not yet." His eyes pleaded with me as he reached for my hand.

I caught myself right before I pulled it away.

"Look. Don't say yes or no. Not yet. Just, I don't know, spend some time with me. With us." He laughed, a short, sharp sound. "That sounds so fucking weird." He sobered again. "Stay for a while, Ailee. And then you can decide." A muscle jumped in his jaw. "If it's too much for you, I completely get it, and I'll totally back off. But"—he scooted his chair closer to me and brushed my hair back away from my face—"I really hope you find out you like having a bunch of new friends all in one hot body." His lips twitched in a tentative smile.

I tried to return it, but couldn't quite manage it.

He swallowed hard. "What do you think?"

I honestly didn't know. "What does your therapist think about this? About...us?"

CHAPTER 17

Tyler

My therapist thought I was fucking crazy.

Or on the verge of a major breakthrough. She couldn't quite decide.

But there was just no way in hell I was giving Ailee up, not if she would stay. At this moment, however, as I stared at her stricken face, I hated myself. I fucking hated myself.

But it wasn't going to stop me. "You know, if I wasn't such a selfish asshole, I would let you go. Maybe not tell you any of this and just let you think you were right all along about me. I'm too young, you're not ready, and whatever the hell else was going through your head when I first let you know how I felt about you. But I'm not that guy, 'lee.

I'm not a good guy. And I don't...I *can't*...picture the rest of my fucking life without you in it. So, if you'll let me, I'm all for dragging you right into this shit with me." I cupped her face and touched my forehead to hers. The sweet scent of her surrounded me, my hands blocked out the rest of the world, and there was only the two of us. "Stay with me, Ailee. Please. Stay."

She leaned toward me, and my heart soared as the weight of the world lifted from my shoulders. I could do this. With her. With my sister. I could learn to live with this fucked up hand life had dealt me.

It all came crashing down around me when she pulled away. Tears spilled down her cheeks as she shook her head. "I can't, Tyler. I'm sorry. I'm so sorry. But I can't."

I sat back in my chair. This wasn't fucking happening. I reached for her again. "Ailee—"

She stood up fast, putting the table between us. "No, Tyler. Don't."

"Ailee—"

But she held up her hand, cutting off whatever the hell I was about to say.

I shut my mouth.

She was leaving me.

Leaving us.

"SHUT. UP." I punched the sides of my head with both fists, wishing I could crush my own skull.

"Who are you talking to?"

It was part question, part accusation. Disgust filled me, leaving an acidic taste in my mouth. I had to get out of there. I didn't want her to see me like this.

Broken.

Tangled up in my own head.

Unable to stand being in my own skin.

Without another word, I got up and walked around, gathering up the rest of my clothes. My jaw ached from clenching my teeth so hard. When I was dressed, I picked my coat up off the floor and shrugged it on.

"Tyler."

I couldn't look at her. "Take care of yourself, 'lee." At the door, I stopped and took a deep breath, looked back over my shoulder one last time.

She was stunningly gorgeous standing there with her horror-stricken face and lush body, the table protecting her from the monster in her kitchen. "This isn't on you," I told her. "It's okay. I really do get it." With one last look, I burned her into my mind.

And then I let myself out of the apartment.

.   .   .

I DID the only thing I could do. Went home. Went back to school. To therapy. Went on with my life.

My therapist, Dr. Bord, was worried about me. Hell, *I* was worried about me. But maybe this was a good thing, in a way. As she so liked to remind me, Ailee may be the light of my dark life—or was—but I'm the one who had to keep that light burning. I had to want to get better for me, not for anyone else.

I didn't care if I got better.

What the hell did that even mean, anyway? How the fuck did anyone get better from this?

Willow was worried about me. She wanted to call our parents. Maybe have them come up. But after I all but threatened to disappear out of her life if she did, she finally relented. I would call them when I was ready, and not a damn minute before. My foster mom, especially, would feel guilty about all of this. I didn't want that on her. She was a great mom. It wasn't her fault I'd turned out like this. I'd probably be even worse if it wasn't for her and my dad.

When that plan didn't work, Willow wanted me to come stay with her. I shut that one down real quick. Snickers and I were just fine here on our own. We'd managed to survive this long, and I didn't need my big sister hovering over me all of the time. I needed the solitude of my own home.

So, I could stare at the walls in peace.

I fell into a routine. School three times a week. Therapy twice a week on my off days. Check-ins with my sister every night. Or, at least, every night I was me. On the nights I wasn't me and didn't call Willow by the specified time, she would call my phone and figure out where I was. We shopped for groceries together on the weekends. Sometimes, I woke up on Monday morning with a fridge full of oranges and little else.

I went through it all on automatic pilot.

On the advice of Dr. Bord, I left my alters notes, trying to open the lines of communication between us. I asked them to fill me in on what happened and where we went and what we did when someone else was "fronting," so I wasn't waking up in strange places in a panic because I'd just lost three or four days. Reminders to pay the fucking bills. But mostly, to make sure Snickers was fed and let out. I wrote down his routine, and my schedule with school and therapy. I applied for aid to help me stay afloat while I made it through school.

And I survived.

I didn't want to, but I did.

Willow popped over every few days to check on me, despite the nightly phone calls. I didn't mind that much. It was better than having her over my shoulder twenty-four/seven, and I knew she was just worried.

"So, what are you going to do about school?"

We were on the couch, watching some bullshit television show. Neither of us really paying any attention to it. "What do you mean?"

"I mean, are you going to be able to graduate with all of this?"

All of this meaning me and my uninvited roomies inside my head.

"The same thing I've been doing. I actually haven't missed that many classes, and Dr. Bord says things will get easier once we all learn to communicate. I could even grow to like having my alters around."

Willow poked me in the gut. "Well, I can tell Tony hasn't been around lately. Your lack of gym time is showing."

I laughed. Actually laughed. I went to the gym regularly to lift, but she was right. Apparently, his boxing regime added a little something to my regular workout routine.

"It's good to see you smile again, Ty."

It felt good to smile again.

I was ready to get better.

CHAPTER 18

Ailee

*I*t'd been three months since I'd seen Tyler. The holidays had come and gone, and we were dead in the middle of the rainy winter my little town shared with Seattle. I really didn't mind it. It kinda fit my mood.

I'd spent Christmas with my daughter, Rachel, out in Oregon, and despite my heavy heart and tendency to burst into tears on a moment's notice, it was really nice. We had snow, and hot cocoa, and we talked. Really talked. A lot.

I'd even told her about Tyler.

Once she'd gotten over the shock that her mom was a woman with feelings and needs just like her, she'd actually been super supportive. She'd handed me tissues when I'd broken down and told her how much I missed him. She'd listened when I'd explained how he made me feel alive again. She'd even talked shit about him with me in an effort to try to make me feel better.

It didn't work. I'd come home to my empty apartment, set down my bag, and got out the ice cream.

I stared at the new photos on the wall of my studio. They were dark. Moody. Nothing at all like my normal stuff. But still beautiful. Objects. Rain. The mountains. Dark things. Mysterious things.

They reminded me of Tyler.

The now familiar ache in my chest made itself known, and I rubbed my tired eyes. I don't think I'd ever been this miserable over a guy before. Even when I'd gotten divorced, I'd been upset that I'd wasted so much of my life with a man who barely knew I was alive. I'd been scared about going out on my own. But mostly, it had been a relief to get from under the dark cloud that had been my marriage.

My cell phone rang. As I walked out front to pick it up from my desk, expecting it to be Stef, I eyed the storm clouds moving in through my large front windows. She'd been bugging me to "get back on the horse" since I'd gotten home from my daughter's, but I had no interest in getting on the horse or anything else. Especially not some strange guy I met in a dark bar.

However, it wasn't Stef. It was a number I didn't know.

I silenced the phone and let it go to voicemail, then went back to my photos. I was trying to decide which group to send to the magazine. They wanted pictures that would make people want to move here. Would tree-covered mountains shrouded in a spooky mist attract people? They'd attracted me.

Two hours later, I had my photos picked out and began to gather up my things to go home. I made a face at the window as I pulled on my weatherproof winter jacket. I didn't think it was going to do me much good tonight. The rain was pouring down outside, and I could already feel its icy fingers soaking me all the way down to my bones.

The screen lit up when I picked up my phone and there was a voicemail from earlier. I listened to it as I walked around, turning off the lights.

"Ailee? Hi. This is Willow, Tyler's sister? Um, he gave me your number a while back...I was just wondering if you'd seen him. He usually checks in with me every night, and I haven't heard from him for two days. Call me back, okay? I'm really worried. Okay. Um. Thanks."

I listened to the message again. And again. Then I stared at the number on the screen, my heart racing, trying to decide if I should call her back or not. If something had happened to Tyler...

If something had happened to Tyler, I'm not sure I really wanted to know. Did that make me a horrible person? These last months had just been so hard, I didn't know if I could handle re-opening that wound. Plus, I hadn't heard from him at all in all that time. If he was having some kind of emergency, I didn't think he'd want me involved. I'd left him. If I showed up now, it would make him think he still had a chance to convince me to stay with him.

Did he still have a chance?

My arm fell to my side as I raised my eyes to the window. I stared out at the rain, not really seeing it.

I'd missed him these last months. I still missed him. And it wasn't getting any easier. However, I still didn't think I could live with his DID. It would take a bigger person than me to be with someone like Tyler. But, the least I could do was call Willow back and let her know I hadn't seen or heard from him.

I hit redial and took a deep breath as I lifted the phone to my ear.

"Hello?" Willow answered on the first ring. "Ailee?"

"Hi," I said.

"Oh, my God, thank you for calling me back. Have you talked to Tyler at all recently?"

Something was in my throat, and I had to clear it before I could answer her. "No, I haven't. I haven't talked to him since—" Since he told me. "Um, not for a couple of months. I'm sorry."

I could hear the tightness in her own throat. "Okay. Thank you for letting me know." A pause. "If he does happen to get in touch with you…"

"I'll let you know. I promise." I started to hang up, but stopped before my finger hit the button. I lifted it back to my ear. "And, would you do the same? Please? Just so I know he's okay."

"Yeah," she told me. "Of course. Thanks again."

Later that night, I'd just gotten snuggled up in bed with the remote for the TV when my phone rang again. "Hello?"

"Ailee, it's Willow. I found Tyler." She broke off, and I could hear her talking to someone. "Sorry. I'm getting in a Lyft."

"Is he all right?"

"I don't know. He's in the hospital. He's been there since yesterday, but he didn't have his card or his wallet, so they didn't know who to call. He's hurt. I'm heading there now."

I threw off the blankets. "What hospital?"

"The one in Bellevue, closer to you."

"I'll meet you there." I hung up the phone and threw on my clothes from earlier, adding a gray pullover hoodie over my jeans and pulling on boots that would keep my feet dry. Grabbing my coat and keys, I locked up and ran down to my car, my chin tucked to my chest in an effort to keep the constant rain out of my face. There was no way in hell I was waiting for a bus right now.

I hadn't driven it in so long it took me a minute to figure out how to make it work. Or maybe it was just the panic rising inside of me, making my hands shake. I finally got the engine turned over and sent a heartfelt thanks up to the sky that it was full of gas. Somehow, I managed to tamp down my fears and concentrate on the road just enough to get me onto the highway without ramming into anyone.

Halfway to the hospital, I had a thought. If Tyler had been in the hospital, who was taking care of Snickers?

I changed lanes, heading to Seattle. It wasn't until I was inside his building and standing in front of Tyler's apartment that I realized I didn't have a key to get in. "Dammit!" My fist came up, and I punched the door, hard enough to bring tears to my eyes. "Dammit!!" All of the fear and pain and loneliness bubbled to the surface, overwhelming me in its intensity. I leaned my forehead against the door and let the tears overflow. There was no denying it; I had feelings for him still. Big, huge, ugly feelings. It wasn't just that I was lonely, because I hadn't been lonely before he came around. I'd been just fine. As a matter of fact, I'd really enjoyed my independence. Something I'd never had before.

A glance up and down the hallway assured me no one had seen my outburst. I sniffed and wiped my face with my hands as I tried to get myself together. I wasn't helping Snickers or Tyler by falling apart outside his apartment. Maybe I could find a manager or someone who would let me in.

I walked out of his building and went around the side. Luckily, the rain had lightened up to a fine drizzle again. Maybe there was a back way in. I could check his back-patio door first. One large fence line ran around the perimeter at the back of the building. It was old, and halfway rotted in a lot of places. I peeked through a hole in the slats about where I figured Tyler's place was.

Snickers huddled beside the door, waiting for someone to let him in, trying to stay dry. "Snickers!"

He heard me, for his little head popped up and he zeroed in on my location. He barked a few times but didn't leave his spot. Poor guy must be freezing.

"Hang on, buddy. I'm coming to get you." I followed the fence line and found a gate with a padlock on it. "Shit." I kept going through the muddy yard, being very careful not to think about the reason I was there. My focus was on getting to the dog, and only that. Once I had him safe and warm in my car, I'd think about the next step.

Around the corner on the opposite side of the building, I found a section of fence where a group of loose boards were just kind of shoved into the spot they should be, the top half leaning out toward me. With a good tug, they came free of the wet ground. It wasn't wide enough for me to get through, but I was pretty sure I could get Snickers out if I could get him over here.

I started calling him, adding some whistles for good measure. It took a few tries, but I finally saw his little, brown body come inching toward me in the dim light of the streetlights behind me. "Come on, boy!" I called. "Come on, Snickers! You wanna come with me? Come on, big boy!" I kept calling until he was close enough to see who I was. "Come on, buddy! Come on!"

He came running then, stopping only for a second when he hit the fence before wiggling his little body through and out the other side to me. Whining happily, he jumped up to great me, coating the front of my pants with muddy paw prints.

"Hey, boy," I greeted him as I pet his wet head and bent down for some puppy kisses. He was shivering from head to toe. "Come on. Come with me."

I didn't have a leash, but I didn't need one. He followed me right to my car, jumping into the back of my Toyota like he'd done it a million times. He sat politely in the back, his little body shaking. I got into the driver's side and cranked up the heat.

"Okay, let's go see what's going on with your daddy. We'll grab you a snack on the way."

Thirty minutes later, I pulled into the hospital parking lot. I cracked the front windows just enough to let in some fresh air and left my coat and some French fries in the back with the dog to keep him warm. I'd already given him some water. Not the healthiest meal, but the poor guy was starving. "I'll be right back," I told him. "Stay."

Luckily, I'd found a parking spot pretty close to the door, so I didn't get majorly soaked as I pulled up my hood and ran across the lot. Inside, I went to the information desk. My voice shook as I asked the nurse, "Tyler Hale's room, please." I had to spell his last name twice before she said, "Room 402."

I thanked her and made my way to the elevator. Tyler's room was on the left at the beginning of the hall. The door was ajar. I stopped, unable to bring myself to go in. I guess I was still on the fence about whether or not I should. I wanted to make sure he was okay, but I could just call Willow to get that information. And I could also tell her to let him know I have Snickers and he's fine.

So, why had I come?

I stepped closer. I could hear voices now. Tyler's and his sister's. He sounded upset, and she was telling him to calm down, that she promised she would go check on "him" as soon as she left the hospital.

I opened the door and walked inside, slowly making my way into the room. The curtain was pulled partially around the bed, the foot the only visible part. There were two leg-shaped lumps beneath the blankets. Willow sat in a chair on the other side. She had pulled it up to the bed and had one hand on what I assumed was Tyler's ankle.

When she saw me, she stood. Her blonde hair was pulled up in a wispy bun and she was dressed much like I was. Her eyes were red and swollen. "Hey. I didn't know if you were coming." Her eyes dropped to the muddy paw tracks on the front of my jeans. "Did something happen?"

"I stopped to check on Snickers."

"Ailee?" The lumps beneath the blanket moved, and Willow frowned and rushed to the head of the bed where I couldn't see her anymore.

"What are you doing, Tyler? Get back in bed!"

"I want to see her."

I stepped closer, until I stood at the edge of the curtain and could just see behind it. My heart was pounding and my hands were shaking, and some sick part of me was almost glad this had happened so I had an excuse to see him again.

Tyler was sitting up, holding his head with one hand. The other was white knuckling the sheets. He was wearing a hospital gown. It exposed his strong back and the top of his fine ass. There was a purple bruise over his left kidney.

His sister stood in front of him, hands on his shoulders, trying to force him to lay back down. When she saw me there, she said, "See? She's right here. Now, lay down!"

He twisted around, and I gasped when I saw his face. It was so swollen and discolored I barely recognized him. One eye was nearly swollen shut. His upper lip was cut. He had stitches above his left eye and on his cheekbone. He didn't say anything. Just ran his eyes over me, much like I did to him.

I came to the foot of the bed, and he laid back, jaw clenched and one arm around his ribcage. Willow helped him get his legs back on the bed. He was wearing socks, those slip-proof ones hospitals give you.

"I have Snickers," I told him. "He's in the car."

"Is he okay?" Tyler asked. "I, uh...I didn't leave him. It was Tony. One of the alters. He's normally really good about taking care of him, but...I don't know, something happened. He was upset. And as you can see, he took it out on me." He waved a hand over his body. "Or rather, whoever the hell it was he'd decided to challenge to a fight. I really wish he'd stick to punching bags."

I nodded, unsure what else to do.

"Ailee? Is he okay?"

"Oh, uh, yeah. He's fine. A little cold and hungry. He's wrapped up in my coat on the backseat with some French fries." I held up a hand. "I know it's not good for him. I'll get him some dog food. Just let me know what kind."

Tyler stared at me long and hard. "Willow, would you leave us alone for a few minutes?"

"Sure," she told him after a pause. "I'll go get some coffee."

She gave me a small smile as she left. "Thanks for stopping for him."

"You're welcome."

And then I was alone with the man who had changed me forever.

CHAPTER 19

Tyler

She's here.

I never thought I would see her again, but she was really here. It'd been three months since she told me she couldn't handle being with me. Three fucking months of feeling like I'd been kicked in the chest. I'd never been happier to see anyone in my entire fucking life. And at the same time, I felt a wave of pure anger.

If I had only known that *actually* being kicked in the chest would get her to come see me, I would've done it myself weeks ago.

A tear slid down her cheek.

"Don't cry, sweetheart." Ah, God. She was killing me. "Ailee, come here." I held out my hand. My ribs screamed in protest, but my body fucking ached for a completely different reason. A part of me hated her for doing what she did, and still, I needed her close to me.

She wiped at her damp cheeks, looking everywhere but at me. "I just wanted to see how you were. Willow called looking for you and told me she hadn't heard from you for a few days. I was on my way here when I thought about Snickers."

"Thank you for going to get him. I've been going crazy lying here. I didn't know if he was in the apartment or outside or what."

"He was outside."

"Ah, fucking hell." I closed my eyes. The poor little guy. I was a horrible fucking dog owner. I should find him a new person. One who wasn't living with other people inside of him. When I opened my eyes again, I had to squint against the pain for a few seconds before I could focus on Ailee. She had moved a bit closer, but still not quite within reach.

"He's okay," she assured me. Her voice was thick with the tears she was trying to hold back. "How did your sister get my number?"

I had to think about that for a minute. "I gave it to her when we were...before everything happened." Just in case. "I'm sorry, I should've told you. That was shitty of me to do without permission. I just wanted her to have it in case I lost time again and she was looking for me." I gave her a small shrug. "She's the only family I have here." *Other than you.* I didn't say it out loud, but actually, Ailee was more than family to me. She was the love of my life. Even now. Even when I wanted to hate her.

"Knock, knock."

I tore my eyes from the beautiful woman in front of me to see Dr. Bord entering my room. Perfect fucking timing.

"Hi," she said. "I just wanted to check on you." As per the usual, she didn't call me by name, allowing whoever was fronting to make themselves known.

"I feel like I was dropped from a plane without a chute, but it looks worse than it is," I told her. I gestured to Ailee. "This is Ailee. Ailee, this is my therapist, Dr. Bord."

The ladies shook hands. "So, *this* is Ailee." Dr. Bord smiled. "It's nice to finally meet you."

Ailee glanced at me with a strange look, almost hurt, then turned back to the doctor. "You, too," she told her. "I can go—"

"No," I told her. "No. Don't go anywhere."

"But, if your doctor wants to talk to you—"

I turned to Dr. Bord. "Ailee can hear anything we have to talk about." What the fuck was I doing? I should just let her leave. She obviously didn't want to be here.

Dr. Bord smiled. "Actually, Ailee, if you had any questions, now would be a great time to ask them. Just let me close the door."

Ailee turned to me, her expression filled with panic and something else. Hope? Curiosity? "Why would she think I have questions? I'm not in your life."

Ah, sweetheart. But you are. Even if I never see you again, you'll always be in my life.

My therapist returned and pulled up a chair. I moved my legs, with some effort, so Ailee could sit on the side of the bed.

She looked back and forth between us a few times, then sat.

I wanted to take her hand. To touch her. Pull her down across my chest so I could feel the weight of her body and smell her hair. And fuck my broken ribs.

But I was angry. I was angry at Ailee. Fucking pissed off that she didn't have the balls to stay with me. To fight for me. Angry that she had the fucking nerve to show up here. Now. When I'd just finally gotten to a point that I didn't ache for her every second of every day.

A week ago, I was ready to go on with my life. Ready to come at this thing with both fists. Handle this thing on my own. Learn how to live with my diagnosis. And I still was. I felt good. I felt strong. Well, except for all the cuts and bruises and that. But that shit would heal.

And now she was here, and I couldn't take my eyes off her.

She could give me her excuses, feel her fears, whatever. She was here.

She was fucking here.

And if I had a chance to get Ailee back, I was gonna take it. I didn't need her to forget my problems anymore. But I wanted her in my life. If I got the slightest fucking inkling from her that she wanted the same thing, I would be an idiot not to convince her to stay this time.

"So, how are you feeling, Tyler?" Dr. Bord asked. "In here," she added, tapping her head. "How's your headspace since this happened?"

"Good," I told her. "The same."

"No new progress?"

"Not yet," I said.

Ailee stared down at her hands.

"Dr. Bord and I are trying to 'open the lines of communication' between myself and the other alters," I told her. "So far, all we've managed is to leave notes for each other. It helps, but it would be better if we could talk in here." I tapped the side of my head, much like the doctor had just done.

"What we're aiming for is System Coordination," Dr. Bord told her.

Ailee raised her head. "You want them to talk to each other. Work together."

"Exactly," she told her.

"Is there a cure for this?" The words burst from her, loud and a little bit angry. A flush crept up her neck to her face. "I'm sorry. I didn't mean for that to come out so loud."

But my therapist took it in stride. "Depends on what you mean by a 'cure.' Our goal is to improve Tyler's life functionality, not really to get rid of the alters. At least, not until they're ready to go." Crossing her legs, she leaned forward and rested her weight on her forearms. "Anything else you'd like to know? I can't discuss everything, but I can do my best to make being with him as easy as possible."

Ailee glanced at me again.

"She's not with me," I told Dr. Bord.

"Oh, I'm sorry. I assumed since you were here..."

"Willow called me. I just wanted to make sure he was okay." And with that, she stood. "I should go."

"Ailee, wait."

"I can keep Snickers with me until you get out of here..."

"Ailee..."

"It was nice to meet you, Dr. Bord." With a small smile in my direction and a steel rod jammed down her spine, she started walking toward the door.

"Ailee! Fucking wait a minute!"

I heard her footsteps stop abruptly, but she didn't come back.

"Can I catch up with you later?" I asked Dr. Bord.

She gave me a knowing smile. "Of course. But I'll see you soon. And don't stress yourself out."

"Absolutely."

After she left, Ailee wandered back toward me until I could see her again. "Tyler, I don't think there's anything to say here."

"Then why did you come?"

"What?"

"Why the hell are you here, Ailee?" Her trying to walk out on me like that had totally set me off. Not that I expected her to see me all banged up and have a complete change of heart, but I did expect...I don't know...something. "Are you just trying to fucking torture me?"

That got her attention. "No, Tyler. That's not what I'm doing." Her voice had an edge to it.

"What are you doing, Ailee? I mean, I appreciate you helping Snickers. You know that. But you could've just taken him back to your place and called. So, I'm going to ask you one last time." I paused for a breath, preparing myself for her answer. Good or bad. "Why are you fucking here? And please don't give me anything other than honesty. I'm fucked up enough as it is."

She didn't answer, just stood at the edge of the curtain near the foot of the bed, head down.

"Ailee!"

Her head snapped up. Tears streamed down her cheeks. "I wanted to see you."

She was ripping my fucking heart out. "Why?"

She dropped her head again.

"Why, Ailee?" My lungs ached. I couldn't breathe. She looked so defeated, standing there twisting her hands, looking at the floor. "Fucking tell me."

With a sniff, she raised her head, and her blue eyes— bright with tears and something else I couldn't identify— sought mine. "Because I miss you." She was shaking her head before I could respond. "I miss you so much, Tyler. But I don't know how...I don't..."

She was killing me. Fucking killing me. I reached for her, gritting my teeth against the pain. "Ailee, come here."

She shook her head.

My arm fell back to the bed, and I slammed my head into the pillow. "What do you want from me, Ailee? Huh? I'm doing everything I can here."

Silence greeted my question. And then, "I just want to be with you." The words were spoken so softly, I barely caught them.

I raised my head.

She was staring at me, her beautiful face a mask of pain, tears flowing down her cheeks. "I just want to be with you, Tyler."

Pain tore through me as she cracked open the hole in my chest with only words, even as the slightest light of hope filled it. "Then be with me, Ailee. *All* of me. Just...be with me."

She wiped at her face, but it was a losing battle.

"Please, come here. Or you're going to force me to hurt myself getting out of this bed to come to you. Because I can't lay here a fucking second longer and not touch you." I raised my arm, offering her my hand.

Stepping toward me, she took it.

Such a small connection, but I felt the touch of her fingers all the way to my bones. It was *something*. I wrapped my fingers around hers. "I'm so sorry, 'lee."

She frowned. "It's not your fault you're in here."

"Not for that. I'm sorry I dragged you into this mess that's my life. I'm sorry I'm not a normal guy. You deserve normal."

She shrugged. "I had normal. It was boring."

That hope in my chest brightened a little bit more. "What are you saying?"

It took her a long time to answer. "I'm not exactly sure, to be honest. I just know I've been...not happy without you around."

"Well, I've been fucking miserable," I told her. "But it was a good thing for you to send me away."

Her eyes found mine. "Why do you say that?"

"Because I needed that time to get my head together. So to speak."

Ah, a smile. It was small and teary. But it was there.

"Having a chance with you was the best fucking thing that ever happened to me, that happened at the worst possible time. I wanted to be with you all the time, so I could forget about all this other stuff going on with me. Or, at least, try to. However, when you left me, I had to face it head on. It forced me to swim or drown. I chose to swim. And I did it for me. Not anyone else."

"So, what does that mean?"

"It means I still want to be with you all the time, but now my only motivation is to get you naked in my bed." I meant it as a joke—kind of—and it worked.

Her laughter was one of the best things I'd ever heard, second only to her moans when I was deep inside of her.

I squeezed her hand, tugging her a little closer, and took her other hand. "Look at me, Ailee." When her eyes met mine, I laid it all out there. "I know it's not going to be easy. There's a lot of shit going on here. And I'm not going to lie and pretend there isn't. But this thing between us, 'lee, it doesn't happen all the time. It's fucking rare." I didn't want to say this last part, but it was something that needed to be said. "If you don't want to deal with my baggage, I stand by what I said at your apartment. I get it. I totally do. And I wouldn't blame you. But, I'm asking you, Ailee, to give this a chance. Give us a chance. Because I fucking ache for you. Constantly. Just to look at your face. Or feel the touch of your hands on me." I rubbed my thumbs over her knuckles. "To hear your voice."

She sank down onto the bed next to my hip, her shoulders falling forward.

"Ailee."

She turned her head, her eyes meeting mine.

"I'm asking you to stay with me. *Be with me.*"

"What about the rest of the people in your head?"

"I don't know," I told her. "That's something we'll have to work on."

My heart splintered into a million little pieces as I waited for her answer, but I'd said all I could say. I couldn't push her anymore. This had to be her decision. Her choice. Life with me would be interesting, to say the least, and it wouldn't be easy. But I couldn't imagine this woman not being in it.

Turning toward me on the bed, she laid one hand on my thigh, and even in the condition I was in, a shot of lust shot straight up into my cock. But I ignored it. That wasn't what was important right now.

"Okay," she said.

It took me a minute to fully comprehend what she was saying. "What?"

"I said okay," she repeated. "Let's do this, Tyler."

And my splintered heart rapidly became whole.

EPILOGUE

Tyler

I sat at my kitchen table and watched Ailee as she unpacked a bag of groceries she'd brought over. Snickers danced around her feet. She was making dinner.

We were taking things slow.

It'd been three weeks since I'd gotten out of the hospital, and I was making great progress with my therapist. We now knew of five alters:

Kate, who wanted to get into interior design and liked movie dates with Ailee.

Miko, a younger guy who liked art and techno music. And oranges. He fucking loved oranges. He'd also met Ailee that day he and Willow were shopping. He wanted to hang out with her some more, but she made him nervous because he thought she was really pretty.

The guy had great taste.

Tony liked to take out his aggression through boxing. He was also the silky boxer wearer and could watch reruns of Mash for days on end.

Superman was just a kid. Though he had fronted when I was younger, these days he felt safer just staying inside the system.

And Samuel. We didn't know much about him. Not yet. But I had a feeling he was a pretty heavy dude. Not physically. Mentally. My therapist thought he might know some things that I probably wasn't ready to handle right now. And that was okay. He'd make himself known when it was time.

Apparently my alters had been there for a while, living quietly within the system, or inner world, that was my head. We didn't know what triggered them, or why they'd suddenly started fronting, but they were here now, and that was okay.

"How does spaghetti sound?"

I smiled at the sexy woman in my kitchen. "It sounds great, sweetheart."

She smiled and came over to give me a kiss. Something she didn't do until she knew who she was kissing.

I pulled her down onto my lap, tugging her in close so I could nip at the soft skin of her neck. "I love you, 'lee."

She stilled in my arms. Fuck. Maybe it was too soon.

Pulling away, she took my face between her hands. "I love you, too, Tyler."

"All of me?"

One side of her mouth turned up in a teasing smile. "We're working on that."

"Well, let me help you out." I stood up with her in my arms and took her back to the bedroom.

Dinner was gonna have to fucking wait.

THANK you for reading Tyler and Ailee's story! If this is your first book of mine and you're ready to read more, AND you love dark mafia romance, start with:

His Game (His Obsession Trilogy Book 1)

ABOUT THE AUTHOR

Hi! My name is Angel Rayne and I write dark, delicious romance with antiheroes who would burn down the world to save the woman they love. I never understood why the villains never win the girl, and so I decided to write them their own love stories where they do.

Here are a few other odds and ends about me...

-Music inspires my stories and I make playlists for every book.

-I am not a fast writer. My stories take time to write. They need to brew in my head. To have book releases close together I have to write ahead. But I would much rather take the time the stories need to be the best they can be than try to rush them out. Trust me on this one.

-I love the rain, and I'm happiest when I'm sitting in a coffee shop with my laptop as it storms outside.

-I prefer to go watch movies alone, with one of those fancy coffees hidden in my purse. (Yes, I really do this.)

-My husband calls me his "little bird" because anything that sparkles catches my eye.

-I will never have enough soft blankets. Ever.

-I love ALL THE DRAMA...but only in books.

-I will forever re-watch The Phantom of the Opera with the hope that by some miracle, this time Christine will choose the right guy.

Thank you for reading my stories, and I always love to hear from you! You can reach me at: angel@angelrayne.com